GALE
CENGAGE Learning

Copyright © 2009 by Elisabeth Hoorweg.
Thorndike Press, a part of Gale, Cengage Learning.

ALL RIGHTS RESERVED
All the characters in the book are fictitious, and any resemblance to actual persons, living or dead, is purely coincidental.
Thorndike Press® Large Print Gentle Romance.
The text of this Large Print edition is unabridged.
Other aspects of the book may vary from the original edition.
Set in 16 pt. Plantin.

LIBRARY OF CONGRESS CATALOGING-IN-PUBLICATION DATA

Rose, Elisabeth, 1951–
    Outback hero / by Elisabeth Rose.
        p. cm. — (Thorndike Press large print gentle romance)
    ISBN-13: 978-1-4104-2630-7
    ISBN-10: 1-4104-2630-0
    1. Women singers—Fiction. 2. Australia—Fiction. 3. Large
type books. I. Title.
PR9619.4.R64O98 2010
823'.92—dc22   2010005795

Published in 2010 by arrangement with Thomas Bouregy & Co., Inc.

Printed in the United States of America
1 2 3 4 5 6 7 14 13 12 11 10

OUTBACK HERO

OUTBACK HERO

ELISABETH ROSE

THORNDIKE PRESS
A part of Gale, Cengage Learning

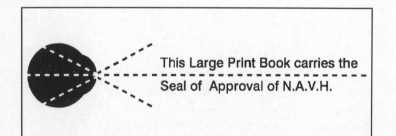

This Large Print Book carries the Seal of Approval of N.A.V.H.

GALE
CENGAGE Learning™

Detroit • New York • San Francisco • New Haven, Conn • Waterville, Maine • London

To Colin, Carla, and Nick

Thanks to my father and Carla for reading the manuscript and making helpful suggestions, such as adding kangaroos.

CHAPTER ONE

When Stella Starr walked into the hotel bar, Jonathan thought he must have been having the equivalent of an Elvis sighting. Not that Stella Starr had passed over to the other side, just gone AWOL. No one knew where she was except, presumably, her. And now Jonathan.

If it *was* Stella, she'd dyed her hair dark brown.

Couldn't possibly be her. Not here, out the back of beyond.

Whoever she was, the girl had a confident stride and moved with the grace of a dancer, held her body straight and her head up. She'd pulled her hair back into a ponytail, which bobbed and swayed as she perched herself on a bar stool and waited for Leo to bring her drink.

Shapely bare legs entwined themselves around each other. A dust-streaked, high-heeled sandal dangled from one elegant foot. She looked hot and tired, melting around the edges, as if she'd traveled a long distance, which she must have done to be sitting in the Central Hotel, Koologong.

This place would be a disappointment. Leo's air-conditioning struggled at the best of times, and now was not one of those. The temperature had hovered around 102 degrees for the last week, and she was many, many miles of red, dusty road from anything cooler. What she was doing, Stella or not, in Koologong, last stop on the way to nowhere, Jonathan couldn't imagine.

Grandpa, asleep in one of the elderly lounge chairs in the far corner, gave a grunting, snoring snort. Easy to forget the old bloke was there when he was asleep. Different story when he woke up.

Startled by the animal-like noise, she glanced around the otherwise empty, dim, shadowy room. Leo had permanently pulled all the blinds against the heat and glare from outside. Her passing gaze caught Jonathan's eye. He nodded and gave a cool half smile of greeting. She stared for a moment, then smiled quickly before turning away, leaving him blinking and dazzled by the change the smile had made to the already pretty face. She'd looked sad when she came in, lonely, despite her innate self-possession. It was something to do with her eyes, that impression of sadness.

"Here you are, love," said Leo. Political correctness had bypassed him, as had sexism and the whole women's liberation movement. Not up on the doings of celebrities either. He placed a brimming glass of iced lemon squash in front of her. A trickle of condensation slid down the side. "Warm one today. This'll cool you down."

"Thanks."

"Leo's the name. Owner and manager of this fine establishment. Passing through, are you?" Leo leaned substantial arms comfortably on the bar, ready for a good interrogation session. The woman's shoulders stiffened slightly, then relaxed. She picked up the glass. Ice tinkled.

"I thought I was, but my car's not sounding happy. I left it at the garage. So I may be staying after all." She didn't offer her own name, and the expression on her face as she uttered the last sentence made it very clear she wasn't seriously considering a night in town a desirable likelihood.

"If you need a bed for the night, we've got plenty of top rooms empty upstairs. All with verandas and air-conditioning and a private bathroom." Leo's expansive tone made the well-worn town pub sound like the Hilton

11

on an off-season weekend.

"Thank you." She took a delicate sip.

"By 'air-conditioning' he means a ceiling fan, which may or may not work, and if you step onto the veranda, either you or it will fall off," put in Jonathan. "Probably both." Two faces swung toward him. Her pretty one, surprised and perhaps amused, Leo's ordinary one, annoyed. "And the bathroom's only 'private' because no one else is staying here."

"Take no notice of him. He's the town grouch. Never stops complaining." Leo turned to Jonathan. "Leaving, weren't you?"

"No. I haven't finished yet, mate." Jonathan grinned and lifted his glass to show the two centimeters still to be drunk.

The woman looked uncertainly from one to the other. She licked her upper lip. "The mechanic said to call back at about five."

"You'll be lucky." Leo gave the bar a swipe with a cloth so she'd think he was a busy man.

Jonathan drained his glass. Nothing happened in Koologong. In fact, she was the most interesting occurrence in the last seven days, and that was only because, the week before, Ted Graham had won a hundred and four dollars in the Lotto and bought everyone around of drinks. Otherwise it would

12

be in the last six months.

The woman offered a tentative smile and put her glass on the counter. Jonathan stuffed the papers he'd been reading into his slim leather satchel, picked up his battered, sweat-stained hat, eased himself out of his chair, and sauntered over.

"Same again?" asked Leo, eyebrows raised in hope.

"No, thanks, better get back to the office. See what's new." He smiled at the girl, who was watching him curiously but pretending not to. "Afternoon."

"Hello."

There came the smile again, dazzling him with even white teeth and a mouth devoid of lipstick but needing none to enhance the lusciousness of the full red lips. Jonathan blinked in astonishment. An unforgettable smile. She couldn't *really* be who he'd thought she was, could she? Didn't she live in Sydney or LA?

"You remind me of someone," he said. *Someone on a CD cover back at the house.* "Have we met?"

She shook her head. The ponytail bobbed and jiggled again. A thin line of perspiration shone above her upper lip. "No. I'd have remembered." Distant and decidedly unfriendly.

13

Jonathan smiled. It was her, without a shadow of doubt. He'd fallen in love with her voice even before he'd seen her face. Deep and warm and sexy despite her youth. She was fifteen, he, seventeen. He'd followed her career haphazardly ever since, never quite losing his adolescent crush. The photo on her most recent CD clinched it. But here in Koologong? Alone? He stuck out a hand.

"Jonathan Knight. Jon."

A slight hesitation before, "Susanna Starkey."

Going incognito, using an alias and all. Why? What had happened to make her run from her ever-so-comfortable world? Her grip was firm, however, and she looked him straight in the eye with a direct gaze from her deep brown eyes. Even in this heat she seemed cool and untouchable. Aloof.

"Nice to meet you, Susanna." He barely managed to let her warm, soft hand slip from his own callused palm. She picked up her glass and drank. His mind went into overdrive.

What a sensation! He listened to the news, read the papers — a day or two out of date sometimes, but still. Stella Starr had disappeared ten days ago, telling her manager she wanted some time off after a messy

14

divorce. Now she popped up in Koologong, eight hundred kilometers and the rest from Sydney and a hundred from the nearest decent-sized town. Sent from heaven by a kindly God. Sent to save him and, by extension, Koologong, from a slow death by desertion, attrition, and neglect.

Questions leaped to mind.

Where was she heading? Could she be persuaded to stay?

Jonathan planted his Akubra hat firmly on his head as he left the pub and stepped into the glaring heat of the afternoon sun. Flies swooped in an irritating horde. The tar was sticky and soft under his soles as he crossed the road heading for Dan's garage and *Last Petrol for Far Too Long sign* — Dan's idea of a joke. Find out what was wrong with her car first. See if Dan was amenable to stretching out the repair work. He usually managed that adequately enough all by himself, but if he knew the reason . . .

"Who's Stella Starr?" asked Dan with his head inside the bowels of her white Ford hatchback, which was perched in precarious suspension on the hoist. Did Dan understand the intricacies of gravity, balance, and hydraulics?

"A singer." Jonathan drew on his reserves of patience. Dan had never been particularly quick to catch on. Trends, fashion, jokes, news. Always behind the slowest runners was Dan.

"What sort of singer?"

"Started out as a teen pop idol, now writes her own songs. Pop but with some jazz influences."

Dan grunted, and something dropped onto the concrete floor with a crash. Jonathan winced.

"Pick it up for us, will ya?"

Jonathan picked up the spanner and slapped it theater-nurse style into the greasy hand that emerged with fingers outstretched. "Scalpel," he said.

Dan chuckled. "Nah, it's a spanner, Jonno." He continued to chuckle as he wielded the spanner. "Think you'd know a spanner when you saw it. You've got a university degree. Didn't they teach you that? Scalpel's what they use when they chop you open."

Jonathan waited. He should've known better than to crack that type of joke with Dan. The chuckles erupted in periodic bursts, and Jonathan did know better than to try to get any sense out of him until he'd finished wheezing and laughing.

Stella Starr of all people. He couldn't get over it. And wasn't she even more gorgeous in the flesh? She'd look wonderful in their range of cotton garments. If she stayed in town long enough. And if she admitted who she was. And if she was agreeable to acting as his model. Lot of *if*s. She wasn't very friendly. Miss Celebrity needed coaxing. But first things first.

"What's wrong with the car, Dan?"

"Could be the carburetor," came the muffled reply.

"Isn't the carbie under the bonnet?" Even he knew that, university degree and all.

"Yeah."

Useless to ask why Dan was poking about underneath the chassis and loosening or tightening things with a spanner. At least he had the answer to his question. Stella would be here for longer than she expected.

Susanna. He must remember to call her Susanna.

Stella's bare legs in her white shorts were sticking to the vinyl-topped bar stool. It was so hot! Even in the pub. Thank goodness the drinks were cold. She eased herself off the stool and asked Leo for the Ladies.

He pointed. "Just through there, love." A friendly grin creased his plump red cheeks. He looked exactly like Humpty Dumpty. Round-faced and bald with a beer belly trying to escape from his worn blue shirt.

She pushed through the swinging door and walked along the corridor. She hadn't been in a place like this for years, and it was the same as every other country hotel in Australia. The same smell of stale cigarette smoke and spilled beer, the same pale green paint on the walls, the same seasickness-inducing patterned carpet on the uneven, creaky floor.

The Ladies had the silhouette of an elegantly coiffed woman in evening dress stenciled in black on the frosted glass panel in the door. The Gents had a Fred Astaire lookalike in top hat and tailcoat. Stella laughed softly to herself. How many residents of Koologong lived up to those images? Not Dan the mechanic or Leo the barman. She went in humming "Puttin' on the Ritz" under her breath.

When she returned to the bar, the good-looking, fair-haired man was back. The one Leo had called the town grouch. They were in a huddle at the end of the bar and looked up with guilty expressions when the door swished closed behind her. Were they discussing her? Probably. If there was one thing Stella Starr was used to, it was people talking about her and staring at her. But not as Susanna Starkey. A little beetle of alarm scurried down her back.

"Hello again." He smiled a very ingratiating smile. She recognized the expression instantly. It was the one people used when they wanted her to do something for them. But these two hadn't recognized her, she was positive. They'd probably only recently gotten news of last year's election results out here. All the same, it wouldn't hurt to keep her distance.

"Another drink?" asked Leo, and when Stella shook her head, he disappeared hastily through a door marked *Staff Only.*

"I've just been 'round to Dan's garage and asked about your car," said the man.

She'd forgotten his name. James? "Thank you. But why would you do that?" She spoke politely, but the careful way she enunciated the words let him know she wasn't pleased. Unless he was oblivious to such subtlety. He could be quite honestly trying to help, but odd things happened in the outback. There'd been a terrible abduction and presumed murder of a British tourist a few years ago. They never found the body, just the hysterical girlfriend who'd been tied up but managed to escape in the darkness. The culprit was safely locked away, though.

Was she being overly cautious? Unnecessarily suspicious? But a woman traveling alone could be in trouble, and who would know? Not telling anyone where she was going didn't seem quite so clever now. The nearest policeman was probably two hundred kilometers away. That snoring old man wouldn't be much of a witness.

He smiled. "Just being helpful. Save you a walk in the heat."

He'd ignored the edge in her voice, or missed it. Maybe she hadn't quite gotten the nuance right. She'd have to be more blunt, without offending him.

"I really don't need help, thank you." She emphasized the *don't,* accompanying the words with a big smile.

"Your car won't be ready tonight."

Stella stared at him. The smile collapsed. "Why not?"

"Dan doesn't know what's wrong." He actually seemed pleased. "You should stay here tonight. Leo's rooms aren't bad, and the food's pretty good."

Her eyes narrowed. "I thought you had work to do. In some office." *Doing what, for heaven's sake? And where?* There were only about a dozen structures in this so-called town, and only about three of them looked habitable.

He grinned, becoming boyish and extremely attractive all of a sudden. "Just a figure of speech."

She noticed, irrelevantly, that the under-layer of his hair was darker brown. The blond would be from sun bleaching. He didn't look the type to have it professionally streaked. He didn't look like an unhinged rapist/murderer, either. Nor did Leo. The heat must have stewed her brains.

Stella glanced at the clock above the bar. Nearly four-thirty. Maybe she should stay. It'd be an experience, if nothing else. The prospect of driving farther in this stinking heat wasn't appealing, and her imagination was veering into the realms of insanity already. They weren't about to abduct her, and if what he said about the car was true . . .

"Thanks for the suggestion," she said, meaning it this time. "Bye."

She strode across to the outer door and pulled it open. The heat slammed into her like a wrecker's ball even under the shadow of the veranda roof. Those rotten little bush flies pounced. The sun's rays bounced off the road surface and shimmered in the air, making the grocery store-cum-café-cum-post office undulate in gentle waves when she looked across the street. Cicadas sent deafening white noise from the gums farther

21

down the road. Peppercorn trees lining the street drooped, beaten down and defeated.

"Hot, isn't it?" His voice sounded in her ear, making pleasant conversation.

"Goodness, yes!" she replied before she had time to wonder why he was following her and be annoyed again. She flapped a hand furiously as a fly edged into her mouth.

"Got a pool at my place if you feel like a dip. Tonight, when it's cooler."

"Sounds lovely but no, thank you." *A swimming pool? Out here?* "Where do you get the water?"

"Bore water, or pump it up from the river when there're no water restrictions. Could swim in the river, but there are too many leeches, and the odd yabby gives you a nip on the bum when you're not looking. I'm heading home soon if you want to come. Plenty of room at my place, and it's free." He grinned as if that last component would be the clincher.

Stella looked him in his hazel eyes. Either he was unbelievably and naïvely friendly, or she was way too cynical. But she'd rather be safe and cynical than abducted and friendly.

"Thanks for the offer, but I'm quite happy to stay at the pub." There wasn't any choice in town. It was the only hotel.

"Please yourself," he said as she spun around and dived from the shade of the pub's wide veranda into the soupy, heat-drenched air of the street. "The garage is the other way."

His casual voice stopped her halfway across. Stella changed direction. What a hellhole. Her sandals were sticking to the softened tar. A heel embedded itself, and her left foot came right out of the shoe. She stepped onto the road surface, now a hot plate.

"Ouch, ouch, ouch." Hopping about on one foot, trying to keep the burned one off the scorching tar, she bent down and wrestled her sandal free. Strong arms slipped about her waist, and suddenly she was whisked up off the ground and carried to the shaded wooden veranda outside the grocery store.

"Put me down!"

"I am, I am. You're heavier than you look."

"I am not!"

"How do you know?" He studied her with his hands on his hips. His hat had been pushed back on his head, and a lock of sandy hair fell across his forehead. His grin crinkled the skin around his eyes. Impossible to prevent her own smile in return.

"You mustn't be as strong as you look." She shoved her sandal back onto her damaged foot and cringed as her burned sole made contact with the leather.

"You all right, darl?" asked a concerned female voice. They had an audience. How wonderful. "Come in, and we'll run some cold water over that foot."

"It's all right, thank you," said Stella with grim desperation. Everyone wanted to help her. Why? Nothing better to do, probably. But this birdlike little gray-haired woman in the yellow hibiscus-patterned dress wouldn't take no for an answer.

"Don't be silly. You have to take good care of your pretty feet," she said. "Come on."

"May I come too?" asked her rescuer. What *was* his name?

"Haven't you got things to do, Jonathan?" The would-be nurse frowned sternly.

Jonathan. Remember it.

"You've done your Sir Walter Raleigh act. Now leave the poor girl alone. She'll think you're one of those perverts with nothing better to do."

That put him in his place. Stella smirked at him. He smiled and looked as though he was about to object. But he obviously thought better of it, because he said, "See you later, ladies," and he went off into the heat of the afternoon.

Stella followed the bright hibiscuses into the dim, cool recesses of the shop. Old-fashioned and friendly, the shop had a wooden floor, shelves stacked with cans and jars and packets behind the long wooden counter, large jars of colored sweets, a modern fridge laden with drinks, and an ice cream freezer. A little round table with a blue-checked cloth and two chairs indicated the café part.

"I'm Doreen."

"Hello, Doreen. My name's Susanna. Sue."

The alias was finally beginning to come easily, although she hadn't needed to use it much. She practiced it as she drove, yelling it out the open window into the wind at the top of her lungs and laughing hysterically at the crazy feeling of freedom. Ten days and she still felt like a newly escaped prisoner looking over her shoulder for the law to catch up. The fireball of anger had begun slowly to dim.

"Nice to meet you, Sue," Doreen indicated that Stella should go through into the private room behind the counter. "What brings you here? We don't get many visitors."

"I was trying to pass through, but my car

25

made funny noises, so I took it to the garage. Perhaps it doesn't like the heat and the dust. Like me." A major mistake, taking the minor, meandering road to Lightning Ridge. If she'd stuck to the highway, she'd be in a comfortable, air-conditioned motel by now.

"Sit down, darl, and take off your sandal. Let's have a look." Doreen indicated a chrome and red vinyl kitchen chair. She pulled up a second one and hoisted Stella's embarrassingly dirty foot onto her lap, peered at it, and frowned as if she were reading her fortune. Her knees were bony under Stella's heel. "He's my son."

"Who? Jonathan?" *No family resemblance there. The father must have contributed all the height. How had this woman's tiny body produced such a big man?*

Doreen chuckled. "No, the mechanic. Dan. He's a bit on the slow side, but he'll get the job done. Eventually. I think you'll be all right." That made more sense. Dan was whippet thin and bony.

"My foot or my car?" asked Stella. Doreen's mind roamed free in its pasture, it seemed, grazing on topics at random.

"Both."

Doreen lowered Stella's leg and patted her on the knee, which Stella took as a general and motherly sign of affection. She smiled. "Thank you."

"Like a cup of tea?" Doreen bustled to the sink and began filling the kettle before Stella had a chance to answer. She switched it on, then took a plastic bowl from under the sink and let an inch of water trickle in. "Put your foot in this."

"I'd love a cup, thanks." Might as well. What else did she have to do? She could please herself. Just as Jonathan had said, except he hadn't sounded pleased.

Stella put her foot with the throbbing sole into the water, which wasn't so much cool as tepid. She guessed it came from a tank on the side of the house. Warm it might be, but it was still soothing to her burned skin. Red dust floated to the surface and formed a dirty ring inside the basin.

"Who exactly is that man? Jonathan." His eyes had crinkled around the edges when he smiled. His face changed completely then, becoming warm and companionable, solid and reliable.

Doreen chuckled. "Good-looking boy, isn't he?" Luckily she didn't wait for an answer but forged on, scooping tea leaves from a canister into a green teapot as she spoke. "Jonathan Knight. His family owns land just out of town. His father ran sheep and cattle but got into all sorts of trouble." Police raids and court appearances danced in Stella's mind, but Doreen squashed those exciting images. "Debt. Like hundreds of other landowners. A run of bad luck with the weather — we're just coming out of a drought — and the markets. The dollar drops, and the bank steps in and says, 'No more.' "

"So what is he still doing here?"

"He went off to university and got himself a degree in business studies and agriculture, or some such thing. He's convinced the bank he can make a go of cotton. How he managed, I'll never know, but I'm not a businesswoman. I run this little place, but it's hardly on the scale of a factory. I won't break any stock market records." She gave a little trill of laughter. "He and his brother are doing the whole shebang themselves — growing to marketing."

"Cotton? Is that what those crops are?" She'd wondered about the vast stretches of intensely cultivated fields in the area and, yesterday, farther towards the coast too. Neat, endless rows of low, shrubby green plants.

Doreen nodded. "Yours is pretty much the reaction of everyone else, but he's gotten the thing going over the last few years.

There's a partner in Sydney who designs clothes. Lena, her name is, and she's a real uppity miss. A city girl. He met her when he was at university, but she won't live out here. Can't blame her really, can you? But we love it. He's built a factory just out of town to process the crop. You might have seen it as you came in. Have to hand it to him, he's trying real hard to make a go of it."

"Is he succeeding?" Stella sifted through the barrage of information for grain among the chaff. She'd noticed the large warehouse and sheds on the outskirts of Koologong and wondered what they were. The name *Koolwear* had meant nothing to her.

"He employs locals, which is a very good thing. This town is dying a slow death apart from the factory. It's our last hope. Cotton's a tough business, but Jonathan's determined to succeed. He's like a knight on a quest." She giggled and put a thin hand to her breast. "Oh, my! Listen to me! He *is* a Knight. He's our Sir Jonathan."

Stella laughed politely and nodded. Her knowledge of the fashion industry was limited, but from the designers who used to clamor for her to wear their clothes on stage and in public, she knew how cutthroat it was. That, on top of growing the stuff, must

29

be incredibly hard and stressful work.

"Is he doing it alone? Apart from the brother, I mean. What about the rest of his family?"

Doreen poured the boiling water into the teapot and placed it, along with two elegant floral-painted china cups and saucers, on the table. She opened a cake tin and placed several lamingtons on a plate.

"I haven't had a lamington in years!" Stella cried in delight. No treats at all, in fact, because she spent most of her life dieting and whipping her body into shape at the gym. A shape required by Xavier's publicity machine. Big, chocolate-iced sponge-cake cubes rolled in grated coconut did not feature on her menu. She'd put on a couple of delicious kilos since she left.

Doreen shook her head with an expression of motherly concern. "You're too thin, if you don't mind my saying so. Help yourself."

Stella took a big bite. Grated coconut dropped all down her front. "Whoops." She giggled through the sweet, delicious mouthful. Wouldn't Xavier have a fit? And her personal trainer, the dragon lady, Julianne.

Doreen sat down opposite her. She fixed Stella with her a beady gray eyes. "He turned to drink after his wife left him. Died when he drove his car into a train at the level crossing. A real tragedy. It may have been deliberate." She sipped her tea. "No one mentions it."

"Who?" asked Stella, startled. For a moment she'd thought Doreen was talking about Xavier.

"His father."

Stella thought for a moment, trying to sort it out. "Jonathan's father?"

Doreen nodded. "Mary took off with a shearer, and everything went downhill from there. He wasn't much good at farming anyway, Robert — never wanted to live out here but had to follow on from his own father."

"Why?"

"Always did as he was told. Old man Knight was a real terror. The other boy, Keith, married and lives there with his wife, Renata. The daughter, Caroline, ran off as soon as she could. Hitched a ride with a road train and — poof — gone with the wind."

Stella nodded slowly in complete comprehension. Poor Robert sounded much like her, living a life dictated by others, deserting spouse included. And you couldn't blame the girl, Caroline, for getting out — Jonathan's aunt, she must have been.

"And now?"

"Jonathan loves the place with a passion. And the town. He wants to save it and the property and his inheritance. The whole thing is Jon's idea. He's the brains. His brother runs the family farm."

"Can he save it all, do you think?"

"He'll die trying," said Doreen. "And he's got the town behind him. Those of us who are left at least." Sir Jonathan sounded like a cross between Zorro and Superman. Keeping his hand in by saving passing young women from hot tar.

"At the hotel Leo said he was the town grouch."

"He is, in a way. He nags until people do what he wants." Doreen smiled a private little smile.

"Does he, indeed? I see how he could become annoying. He's already tried to get me to stay at his place. I don't know the man from Adam, and he tries to pick me up."

"You're a pretty girl."

"And that makes it all right? Not where I come from. I don't go off with strange men."

"And you shouldn't. But Jonathan's not strange. He's holding this town together."

"He's a stranger to me. I've just been divorced from one man. The last thing I want is another one."

"Footloose and fancy-free." Doreen topped up Stella's teacup. "Like me since Herb died. I don't like to speak ill of the dead, but the devil's got company now."

"Oh, I'm sorry." Although Stella wasn't quite sure what she was sorry for, the bereavement or the fact that Doreen had married the apparently unpleasant Herb.

"He doesn't live there alone, you know. They all share the place."

"Jonathan's aunt and uncle?" Presuming she'd successfully kept track of Doreen's rambling story.

"No, Keith's his brother." Doreen's mind leaped the railings again. "I don't think Jonathan's looking for a wife. He's got a fiancée."

Stella swallowed a smile. "Do you think Dan will have fixed my car?" The way Leo had laughed hadn't augured well.

"Hard to say," said Doreen. "Mechanical things are a bit of a mystery to my Dan. Have another lamington."

CHAPTER TWO

"We have to keep her here," Jonathan said to Leo. He sat on the stool Stella had occupied.

A couple of young hands, jackaroos from the nearest cattle station, stomped in, cursing the heat and drawing Leo away to serve them. A few other locals had taken up their usual places at the tables scattered about the barroom. A murmur of conversation rippled through the stifling atmosphere. The ceiling fans swished relentlessly, moving hot air from one part of the room to another and back again.

"How do you suggest we do that?" Leo said when he came back. "Lock her in a room?"

"No. We have to either make it so she wants to stay herself or make it so she can't leave." Jonathan frowned as he tossed various ploys around in his mind. They had to let her think they didn't know who she was.

If anyone let on, she'd be gone so fast, they wouldn't see her for dust.

"What's wrong with her car?"

"Don't know. Dan said he thought it was the carburetor, but he had it up on the hoist."

Leo gave a shout of laughter. "Don't worry, mate. She'll be stuck here for months."

"Maybe. But I'd like to be a bit more certain. Dan might have a brainstorm and actually fix it."

"Yeah, you're right." Leo chuckled again. "Unlikely, though. He'd need an IQ above room temperature for that to happen."

"We just need to let her see how good Koolwear is, and she'll be as keen as we are." Jonathan thumped his fist on the bar.

"Offer her a job as a model." Leo wiped his towel experimentally on a glass and peered at it, then rubbed again.

Jonathan's head whipped up as the suggestion registered, then he slumped. "She'd never take a job. She's going somewhere. And she's a rich star, remember? She's not exactly impressed by us." The suspicious, wary look she'd given him flashed uncomfortably across his mind. Maybe he'd blown his chance already by coming on too strong.

Leo's brow wrinkled. "But you reckon she

doesn't know you know she's a star. So you could be offering her a modeling job because you think she's good-looking. She is good-looking. She's a honey."

"But," Jonathan explained patiently, "the whole point is for her to model Koolwear because she *is* a star."

"Well, how're you going to manage it if you don't let on you know?"

"That, mate, is the problem."

It sure was. How could he convince her to stay in town long enough to discover what a great product they had here? If only he could get her to have a look at the factory and try on some of the clothes. This was far too good an opportunity to let slip. How often did a celebrity wander into Koologong?

"Get us a beer, thanks, Leo," yelled Colin as he slammed through the door, bringing a blast of furnace-heated air with him. Round-faced Alice and tall, slim Linda from the factory followed him in, both wearing Koolwear blouses and skirts, both with faces red and shiny from the heat.

"Knocked off early?" Jonathan cocked an eyebrow at his staff.

"Lot later than you." Colin grinned. "Where've you been all afternoon? I thought you went to Walgett this morning."

"I'm the boss. I don't have to answer to my workers," retorted Jonathan.

"Slaves, more like it." Linda ran freckled hands through her short red hair. "Haven't you got the air-conditioning fixed yet, Leo?"

"Fans are working, drinks are cold," he said, complacent as ever. "What's your problem?"

Linda rolled her eyes and turned back to Jonathan. "We got that shipment packed up."

"Thanks. All we need is a hundred similar orders, and we'll be laughing."

"Hundred more orders like that and we'll need more staff." Alice heaved herself onto a stool. "Advertising is where it's at. We need someone to do a big feature on us. On TV. Can't Lena do anything? Surely she's got contacts."

Jonathan grimaced. Lena had been on the phone just last night saying she'd been offered a position with a sportswear designer, and, the Koolwear income being what it was, she was seriously considering taking it. After her opting out of their more personal liaison several months ago, her defection came as no surprise.

"Advertising is expensive, and it's hard to get TV or print journalists interested enough to come way out here for a story on farming and clothes. Out of sight of smog they panic and think they're lost." Like Lena.

"Never say die, boss," said Colin. "We'll make it." He raised his glass. "Here's to Koolwear."

"What's Koolwear?" asked a curious voice. "If I'm not interrupting."

Jonathan spun around. Her voice sent shivers down his spine. Shivers of excitement at her voice saying *Koolwear.* He visualized his clothes on that breathtaking body. Marvelous. His fingers still tingled from feeling her skin against his hands as he carried her across the road — his teenage fantasies come true.

Displaying a pleasing and instant grasp of the situation, Alice jumped in. "The best pure cotton clothing money can buy. Hand-made right here in Koologong from locally grown cotton." She indicated her blouse and skirt with an extravagant display of arm gesturing and model-like posturing.

Stella nodded. "I saw the sign as I came into town. Thanks. Sorry to butt in."

She glanced around the group apologetically and flashed a tiny smile. They were staring at her with undisguised interest, especially the ruddy-faced, dark-haired man leaning on the bar next to Jonathan. She knew that look. Every woman alive knew

38

that look. X-ray eyes. This one thought he was Superman.

She moved along to where Leo was chatting with the old man who had now woken up and moved to a stool at the bar.

Leo's welcoming grin revealed a large gap between his front teeth. "Hello, love."

"Excuse me, Leo. Could I have a room tonight, please? My car isn't ready."

"Certainly. You can take your pick as long as you choose room number two."

"Why number two?" Was he setting her up for some sort of country-style joke?

"It's the only one with a bed in it. Comfortable enough to sleep in, anyway." He and the old man laughed. "This is Sue, Grandpa."

"How do you do?"

The old man displayed an almost toothless grin.

"I'm not your grandpa," he said to Leo. Watery gray eyes swung to Stella. "I'm not his grandpa. Silly fool keeps calling me Grandpa."

"He is," said Leo.

"Just wishes he wasn't." Jonathan, right behind her again. Out of nowhere. "Understandably."

Stella gave him a wintry little smile. What did he want? He was always breathing down her neck, and it made her uncomfortable, which was annoying. But he was strong. He'd lifted her effortlessly despite his ridiculous complaint about her weight.

"May I go up now?" she asked Leo. If she ignored Jonathan, he might go away.

"Up the stairs and on the left. Bathroom's opposite. You'll find towels in a cupboard in the hall next to number three."

"Thanks."

"Thirty-five dollars per night in advance. Cash only, sorry. The system's down again. Don't know why I bothered going to the trouble and expense of hooking up; it never works," Leo said.

"Oh! Sorry, I didn't realize." Her cheeks, already scarlet from the walk outside, grew hotter. She pulled out her purse and quickly counted out the money. Had to be careful with her cash — didn't have a lot left. The garage should take a credit card, though, and with any luck she'd be in a bigger town tomorrow, one with ATMs. One night in this hotel would be more than enough. An image flashed into her head of the beautiful, air-conditioned, luxury penthouse apartment waiting for her, empty, in Sydney. Not yet. She wasn't ready to go back yet.

"Do you serve meals?"

"Start at six, finish at eight," said Leo promptly. "Cath has to get home for the kids," he explained.

"Your wife?"

"He hasn't got a wife. Who'd marry him?" scoffed Jonathan.

Stella frowned at his rudeness, but Leo seemed to be used to it, because he said cheerfully, "Don't see anyone hankering after you, mate, and the only woman even vaguely interested keeps well away in Sydney like the smart thing she is."

Hear, hear! Maybe Doreen had been more accurate than she thought. He didn't want a wife.

"Cath's husband works for this tycoon here." Leo indicated Jonathan. "Virtually the whole town works for him. He's the lord of the manor."

The whole town? The population was featured on the town sign on the outskirts. "All three hundred and fifty-three people?"

"Not three hundred and fifty-three anymore," said Leo. "Three hundred and forty-one, and that's counting Grandpa." He roared with laughter.

Grandpa chuckled and wheezed and said, "Where'd you put me teeth?" He leaned closer to Stella, enveloping her in a wave of stale body odor, and whispered, "He steals me teeth and hides 'em."

"Don't bother the guests, Grandpa," said Leo. "Sorry, love, ignore him."

Stella smiled and stepped back. "Thank you."

She headed for the door leading to the corridor with the washrooms and the narrow staircase leading up to the mysteries of the first floor. The steps emitted alarming squawks as she ascended, so she kept one hand firmly on the wooden banister in case her weight proved the last straw to treads weakened to the breaking point under Leo's bulk.

Room number two had a gold numeral on its dark wooden door, held in place by an oversized nail. Stella tried the handle. The door swung open. Leo hadn't issued her a key. She'd have to ask for one, in case Grandpa lived here and was given to late-night rambles. She giggled. Didn't want old age creeping up on her.

The room had the basics. One high, wooden-framed single bed with a blue chenille cover, a solid old dressing table, a matching wardrobe, a straight-backed chair, and one ceiling fan, which swung noisily into action when she tried the switch. White net curtains over a beige roller blind covered the only window. Cool, pale gray linoleum on the floor boasted a round blue mat by the bed. She strode across the room and pulled the curtains aside. The blind went up after several unsuccessful tugs at the cord, revealing a view of the wide wooden veranda, dark in shadow now that the sun had moved to the other side of the building. The sash of the window was low and could easily be stepped over. She pushed the window up and leaned out.

Jonathan might be right about the veranda. She wouldn't be climbing out there in a hurry — unless she couldn't pay her bill. She withdrew her head and plopped down on the bed. The mattress was soft to the point of threatening to swallow her up — like sitting on a marshmallow. Springs squeaked when she moved. The ceiling fan also squeaked, with a monotonous, lopsided rhythm, overhead.

What if her car wasn't ready tomorrow? Today was Thursday. She'd be stuck in this town all weekend without enough cash to pay for more than one night. That's if she wanted to eat. If she didn't want to eat, she could manage two nights. Stella frowned.

Surely Koologong had some sort of cash facility. Doreen, perhaps? But she hadn't brought a checkbook, hadn't even thought of it. Plastic was the way nowadays. Everyone took plastic. Except Leo, with his broken-down connection. What rotten timing. What about the cotton factory? They must be reasonably high tech. They should be able to advance her some cash.

It would mean approaching Jonathan.

She fell backward against the pillow. That man! How he'd smirk. There must be another way. What about Dan at the garage? She looked at her watch. Ten to six. He might still be there. She had to go back anyway; her suitcase was in the car up on his hoist.

Stella investigated the bathroom on her way downstairs. There was a full-sized tub and a showerhead over the bath. A little sign warned against excessive water usage and about not drinking the bathwater. She grinned as she read it. No, she wouldn't be drinking her bathwater but, boy, she'd be in the shower as soon as she returned. Hot shower, clean clothes, dinner, cool drink. Luxury. Relatively speaking.

As soon as Stella disappeared through the door, Jonathan gathered Colin, Alice, and Linda together at a table in a corner, out of earshot of the station hands who'd begun a game of darts with a running commentary from Grandpa.

"Do you know who she is?" asked Jonathan.

"No idea," said Colin. "But she is bee-uu-tiful. Think she fancied me?"

"Not a hope, lover boy," said Linda.

"She's Stella Starr."

"The singer?" asked Alice. "You're joking."

"I'm not. I'm positive. Stella Starr took off about two weeks ago and went bush. All by herself, without even her mobile phone. Not even her manager knows where she is. Papers think she's had a nervous breakdown after her divorce."

"One of those publicity stunts probably," said Linda. "They do that sort of thing all the time when they start to slide down the charts."

"Maybe, but she's not really a pop-chart sensation anymore," said Jonathan. "But whatever the reason, we've got her here. And I reckon we should keep her."

"Like a pet?" Linda wrinkled her brow as if seriously considering the idea. "What does she eat? Does she cost much to maintain?"

"They cost heaps," said Alice. "Rich and spoiled. She'd drive us crazy, and we'd end up having her put down. Or we'd have to turn her loose."

Jonathan's patience gave out. "Shut up,

45

you idiots! Don't you see? She can be our figurehead. She can wear our clothes. Be our advertisement. The whole world will want Koolwear if Stella Starr wears it."

"Isn't there a junior problem, Jon? Stella Starr *doesn't* wear it. Stella Starr has never heard of it," said Colin. "Come to think of it, I've never heard of her. How is that? Such perfection."

"You only listen to country music," said Jonathan. "This woman's famous, believe me. I've got her CDs." And had a crush on her since the age of seventeen.

"Did you see the labels she does wear?" asked Alice. "Shorts, two hundred and forty dollars in Double Bay. T-shirt, one-twenty, same location. And her handbag. Goodness only knows where those sandals came from. Rome? New York? Five hundred plus bucks?"

"Not worth much now — one of them's got tar all over it," commented Jonathan. She was featherlight in his arms, hardly weighed a thing. Smelled delicious too — expensive, subtle perfume mixed with hot body odor. Sexy and exotic and exciting.

"I'm thirsty!" bellowed Grandpa. "Everyone ignores me because I'm old."

"Nobody *can* ignore you, Grandpa," said Leo.

46

"We have to make her see that our product is just as good. Better! It's cheaper for a start, and no one, not even the rich and famous, prefers to pay more when they can pay less and get quality. Also, we're Australian, and that should count for something with her."

"What exactly did you mean, 'keep her' here?" asked Colin. "I'm employed as a manager, not a jailer."

"Wheels are in motion." Jonathan grinned. "Hers aren't, though."

"What's she doing here in the first place?" Linda drained her glass of cola.

"Car trouble. Dan's on the job." As he expected, spontaneous laughter burst from everyone at the table.

"Does she realize she'll be here for a while?"

"Not yet." Jonathan leaned forward earnestly. "It's imperative that no one lets on that they know who she is. Dan had never heard of her anyway, and Leo's onside. I've had a chat with Doreen, so as long as no one blows into town and sees her, we should be all right." He glanced around the barroom. "I don't think anyone else here would know her by sight even if they have heard of her. She's changed her hairstyle and color a fair bit."

"Who's that fat bloke?" yelled Grandpa.

"Leo. He's your grandson," said one of the darts players.

"He's not!" replied Grandpa.

"Why can't we say who she is?" asked Colin.

"Because if she knows we know, she'll clear out so fast, your head will spin. She wants to be anonymous for some reason. She's using a different name."

"What makes you think she'll ever agree to this?"

"She will if she stays here long enough to get to know us and sees how much we need her to help."

"But how will you eventually tell her you know who she is? She won't stay here forever. She'll probably just leave without a word when she's ready." Alice folded her arms decisively across her chest. "The whole idea's crazy."

"I'll sort that out when I have to," said Jonathan.

"I wish I had your faith." Colin shook his head. "Women are unpredictable at the best of times, and pop stars are worse. Put 'em together, and phew!"

Alice stood up. "I'm off home before I get sucked into replying to that and beat you to a pulp. See you tomorrow. Do we tell the

48

others at work?"

"I reckon," said Jonathan. "Then no one's going to blurt something out if they recognize her."

"They're not likely to see her, are they?"

"If I take her to the factory, they will."

"Well, stone the crows!" roared Grandpa. "Look at her. It's Margie!"

Stella stopped dead as all eyes in the bar fixed on her. She smiled. She was used to crowd appraisal, but being taken for "Margie" was a first.

Leo said, "Be quiet, Grandpa. This is Sue. She's a guest in the hotel. Everything all right, love?"

"Looks all right to me," said Grandpa. "Give us a kiss, eh, Margie?"

Stella moved smartly away from his bony hand as it went for her bare thigh. She needed to change her clothes. Shorts weren't suitable attire near lecherous old men. Especially one who thought she was an old flame.

"Fine thanks, Leo. I have to go back to the garage and get my suitcase. I left it in my car."

"I'll come with you and carry it." Jonathan, at her elbow again. How did he do it? One minute he was quietly out of the way in a corner with his friends, and the next he was hovering about, being obsequious. Still, if he wanted to lug her bag in the heat all the way from the garage, let him.

"All right," she said. "Thanks."

If anything, the heat had intensified when they stepped outside.

"Does it get cooler at night?" Surely it must when the sun went down.

"A bit. Where are you headed?"

"Lightning Ridge, to see the opal mines."

"Taking the scenic route?"

She grimaced. "Apparently. I'm really just taking my time. I took this road because it wasn't the highway."

Jonathan nodded. "That's our problem."

She glanced up at his face in profile. Nice, firm lines and a straight nose. "You mean because you're not on the highway?"

"Yes."

"I understand." It was her problem now too.

They walked on in silence. The sun was still well above the horizon, thanks to daylight savings. Stella's shirt stuck to her back. She must smell dreadful. The cleaner of her two dirty feet was fast becoming gritty and sweaty again in the ruined sandal. She urgently needed a shower and clean clothes.

The garage was shut. There was a roughly

printed sign stuck to the door. *We're Closed Because We're Not Open.*

Stella gasped in dismay, which turned rapidly to incredulous anger. "Oh, great! Now what?"

This was too much. No clean clothes, no toothbrush, no shampoo. Maybe Doreen would loan her a floral frock circa 1954 or she could buy some of this man's cotton clothing. No, she couldn't. She had no money.

Jonathan tried the door experimentally. Dan had locked up tighter than the belt around Leo's beer belly. He hadn't meant to stop her from getting at her suitcase; he had just asked Dan to take his time on the repairs tomorrow. He wouldn't be around to open up for her either, because Thursday was his cricket-training night over in Cooper's Creek.

"Do you take credit cards?" Her voice was strained, near to the breaking point.

"Not personally, no." He turned around. Her face was flushed from the heat. She looked so worried and defenseless, he had an almost overwhelming desire to hug her.

"I mean for your clothing, the cotton stuff."

Dimwit! His mind leaped into gear, carnal thoughts replaced immediately by business.

"Yes." Jonathan tried to keep his voice level and his excitement at a minimum. She was going to ask to wear some of his clothes of her own volition. What would suit her? Any of the T-shirt or blouse range, the sundress, three-quarter length pants, shorts — all of it would be stunning on her.

"Could you advance me some cash, please?"

The fantasy fizzled.

"Sorry. We don't carry cash at the factory. It's all mail or online order."

"Oh. Of course. Yes." Stella strode away down the street toward the pub, stumbling a little on the rough surface in her city sandals with the ridiculous heels. But they sure showed off her fantastic, tanned legs in those shorts. She must work out a lot.

"Bit short, are you?" Jonathan caught up to her.

"I can manage. I just didn't expect to have to pay cash at the hotel." She looked up at him, brow creased in annoyance. "It's such a . . . a . . ." She gestured vaguely at the dusty, heat-baked town with its row of tall gum and peppercorn trees offering little relief from the intensity of the sun's rays. "There's nothing! How do you stand it?"

"I love it. It's where I was born and brought up," said Jonathan, stung by her tone and the squashing of the hope that had flared so unexpectedly. "City people don't have a clue. They have no affinity for the country at all. You people expect everything to just appear ready-made and waiting for you to decide what you want. Spoiled," he finished in disgust.

"Maybe." Stella's voice rose in anger. Her eyes bored into his. "But we provide a market for your products. You wouldn't get far if no one bought what you grow, if we all made our own clothes. The same as I wouldn't get far if no one . . ."

"What?" asked Jonathan. "What exactly do you do in the city?" This would be interesting.

She hesitated, looking away. "I'm between jobs at the moment."

"Maybe you'd like a job here," said Jonathan. "Then you'd see what it is we do in this backwater."

"I'm not looking for a job, and if I was, I'd hardly come here," she said, accompanying the words with a tense laugh and sweep of her arm.

Apart from the imposing two-story Central Hotel with its green roof and wide veranda running the length of the upper level, a deserted building with *Arts Centre* faintly discernible over the door, Doreen's store, the garage, and seven or eight weatherboard houses in varying stages of decay, there was nothing but the few trees lining the road. A couple of kilometers out of town on the way in, she'd passed a little church surrounded by gravestones.

The late-afternoon sun streamed relentless bright gold light into her eyes as she walked. Baking her brain. Fuelling her anger. Three young boys on bikes hurtled toward them down the road, with a dog galloping after them. They skidded to a halt in front of Doreen's store, threw the bikes down, and crashed in through the door. The dog stood waiting, panting, tail wagging slowly.

"There are worse places," said Jonathan from behind her. Angry, defensive. "You'd need to go a long way to find a better community spirit, but you wouldn't know anything about that. It's every man for himself in the city. We look out for one another out here."

Stella stopped, furious. She spun around to face him. "You know nothing about me. Nothing at all!"

"I might know more than you think," he shot back.

"What do you mean?" Alarm tightened her throat. She knew nothing substantial about him either. Doreen's ramble was a flimsy recommendation. This man might have a gigantic and uncontrollable temper. He might become violent. She stepped back a couple of paces. Her mind went into self-defense mode as taught by Instructor Brett. Watching. Wary. Consciously relaxed muscles. Ready to move.

Jonathan looked over her head, away down the dusty red road into the distance where the heat shimmered on the horizon in the golden glow of the afternoon. He was as angry as she was. His jaw was clenched in his tanned face, but he suddenly relaxed and smiled down into her eyes.

"I know you're very pretty, you're hot, temporarily strapped for cash, stranded here out the back of Bourke, miles from civilization, surrounded by lecherous, foul-mouthed old men and overly friendly locals, you don't have a change of clothes, and you're probably hungry and tired."

Stella stared at him for a moment, then managed a weak smile. Her anger died abruptly. She nodded, unable to speak because if she did, she'd cry and embarrass both of them. He must have correctly interpreted her collapse, because he said in a much gentler voice than she'd heard him use before, "Why don't you come and stay at my place?" Her head shot up in surprise. He went on swiftly, "I don't live alone. My brother and sister-in-law live there too. Renata can lend you some clothes. I'll give her a call and warn her we're on our way."

"I . . ." What could she say? It was a tempting offer. Very tempting. But . . . was it sensible to accept?

He waited.

"I've already paid Leo for the night."

"He'll refund it."

He stared at her. Thinking she was a cheapskate? Thirty-five dollars was nothing. Thinking she was making excuses? Was she?

"No, it's not that . . . it's . . ."

"You don't know me from a bar of soap," he supplied for her. "Fair enough. Come back to the pub and ask Leo for a character reference. You trust him, don't you? I'll call Renata from there, with plenty of witnesses. All right?"

Stella nodded.

Every eye in the place swung toward them, and the babble of voices subsided as she and Jonathan reentered the pub. Just like walking onstage. She'd always loved that feeling, the aura of tense expectation, the nervous tingling in her stomach as hundreds and often thousands of eager faces watched her, prepared to hurl themselves into the show and lift her along with the music. Then, she and the band and the audience became as one. Here it might be different. Here she was an outsider. An unknown. She had nothing to offer these people. Just herself. Whoever that was.

More people had arrived in their absence. The bar was packed. This was obviously the social hub of the area. Jonathan caught her eye and smiled as he removed his hat. The tanned skin around his eyes crinkled. He had a lot of tiny creases around his eyes — from squinting in the harsh, bright light out here, she supposed. The eyes themselves were green with brown flecks here and there. Attractive. Very attractive. And she liked the way his brown hair had those streaks of bleached blond — naturally from the sun, not a salon, like most of the self-pampering men she knew.

The conversations resumed around them, but the prickling on her neck meant that people were watching from the corners of their eyes. Mr. Mover and Shaker chatting up the stranded female would pass as great entertainment out here. They were probably taking bets on his progress.

Jonathan edged through the crowd to the bar, exchanging greetings with jovial, weather-beaten, outback farmer types as he went. He was well-liked, very popular. Confidence rising, Stella followed closely in his wake.

"Hey, Leo!" he cried, beckoning.

Leo grinned at Stella. "Get you a drink, love?"

"Thanks. Lemon squash, please. Lots of ice."

"Jon?"

"No thanks, Leo. Dan's locked up and left Sue's bag in the car," Jonathan said. "I'm taking her home to my place. She can borrow something from Renata."

Leo nodded. "Silly as a two-bob watch, our Dan. Sorry about that, love, but Renata'll look after you."

"Sue needs her money back," said Jonathan.

"No." Stella shook her head vehemently. "No, it's all right. I used the room and the bathroom. In fact, I'll nip up there again and have a wash before we go, if you don't mind."

"I'll call Renata." Jonathan pulled a mobile phone from his pocket.

"At least have dinner here," said Leo. "Then I won't feel so bad about keeping your money."

The big softie. Stella smiled. She looked at Jonathan. He shrugged and nodded. "Will it stretch to two dinners?" she asked.

"No worries. What would you like?" Leo pointed to a blackboard menu on the side wall.

She scanned the short list. "Chicken salad, please."

"Steak, thanks, Leo," said Jonathan.

"It'll be about twenty minutes."

Stella went upstairs to her room. The decision had been made almost without her realizing. Naturally. The events flowed from one to the other seamlessly. Leo hadn't batted an eye when Jonathan told him she was leaving the hotel with him. Must be all right. He would have stopped her somehow, or at least put up more of an argument for her to stay. He'd done the opposite. Told her Renata would take care of her. Worried about taking the money that was rightfully his.

There was nothing to be concerned about. Country people had the reputation for friendliness for a reason. And she was experiencing that friendliness firsthand. Jonathan had a point when he said city people didn't understand the sense of community in a place like this. Her immediate reaction had been one of suspicion. Thinking he wanted something from her, when what could he possibly want from plain Sue

Starkey?

She must put those thoughts behind her. Not everyone wanted to take advantage of her. As Sue, she had nothing to offer. Jonathan and his friends were just genuinely nice people looking to help someone in trouble. Relax and enjoy it. It probably wouldn't happen to her again.

CHAPTER THREE

"Ready to eat?" Jonathan, lounging against the bar, straightened up as Stella rejoined him. "In the dining room. Through there." He pointed to the opposite side of the room.

Stella's ponytail bounced along in front of him. She walked with a determined tread, her back straight. He took a deep breath and forced himself to concentrate on the main issue at hand, which wasn't her body.

Cath had set a table in the little-used dining room. Most people ate in the bar, but she'd suggested that Stella would be more comfortable eating in the quiet, faded elegance of the designated area. It appeared she was right.

"It's much cooler in here." Stella looked around with a relieved sigh. "And quieter." She pulled out a chair and sat down. Jonathan sat opposite. He poured two glasses of iced water.

A swinging door burst open to reveal Cath

bearing a tray. "Here you are, Sue. You must be starving."

Stella studied her overflowing plate. She'd never seen so much salad in one place outside a buffet. It seemed to contain every ingredient known to man. The chicken was in there along with lettuce, tomato, beetroot, grated cheese, carrot, cucumber, onion rings, celery, strips of red bell pepper, a small dollop of potato salad, corn niblets, and a hard-boiled egg.

"Everything okay?" Cath slid a basket of rolls onto the table along with a butter dish.

"It's magnificent," said Stella for want of other words to describe her meal. "I don't know whether I'll be able to fit it all in, but I'll try." Her stomach regarded Doreen's lamingtons as a distant memory.

"Give us a yell if you want anything." Cath headed for the door.

Jonathan raised the glass of iced water to Stella and looked her in the eye. "Here's to a successful future."

She raised her glass and clinked, meeting his gaze. "Is it in doubt?"

Jonathan shrugged. "It's a tough business, farming."

"I don't know anything about it." Stella picked up her fork and started in on the mountain of food.

"What do you know about?" he asked. "What do you do in the big city?"

"You asked me that before."

"And you didn't answer properly."

"Why are you so interested in what I do?"

"I'm making conversation." He carved a chunk off the sizzling steak Cath had produced. His plate had disappeared under the steak, mashed potato, and a smaller version of the salad on her plate.

"I worked in a shop. A music shop." If she said any other sort, she wouldn't know the first thing about the stock if he started asking questions.

"Interesting. I like music. What do you listen to?"

"Just about everything. How about you?"

"The same." He chewed, deep in thought, then swallowed. "If you're still here on Saturday, we have a karaoke night. Sort of a competition. Winner by popular vote gets a meat tray." He looked directly into her eyes. "Can you sing?"

She forked up potato salad. "I won't be here on Saturday, I hope." She'd slipped straight over his question. Would he notice? "My car should be ready tomorrow, and I want to get to Lightning Ridge."

"Been there before?"

"No, but it sounds really interesting. All

the people living underground. I love opals."

"Yes, but you've picked the worst time of the year to come outback. Couldn't be hotter."

Stella nodded. "I know, but I didn't have a choice about the timing. I had to go now."

She dropped her gaze to her plate; her fork hung poised from her fingers. Remembering.

Her whole life had been spent pleasing other people. Pleasing her mother, pleasing her teachers, pleasing her school friends, pleasing the people she worked for and/or with, pleasing her manager, pleasing her fans, pleasing her boyfriend into becoming her fiancé into becoming her husband into becoming her ex.

Sitting on her cream leather sofa in her immaculate and elegantly furnished Sydney apartment with its two million dollar view of the ocean, newly divorced for three hours and fifteen minutes at the ripe old age of twenty-six, Stella, experiencing what she vaguely recognized as a deep groundswell of anger, decided she'd had enough of pleasing other people. Mark and That Woman were welcome to each other. They could please themselves. They already had.

For the first time in her life she would be **SELFISH.** In capital letters and bold black. No, in gold, sparkling, shining, and proud. She would do exactly as she wished. Her marriage, the newspapers, the insatiable photographers, her manager, Xavier, her publicity schedule, the pressure to produce the goods for everyone but herself, finished. And if anyone asked her to do anything she'd say no. Unless she really wanted to.

Stella placed her fork with careful precision on the side of the plate and took a sip of chilled water. The icy liquid slid down her throat, calming her, cooling her overheated system.

"Problems?" His voice was soft, concerned.

"Yes, but they're . . . private. Not your business." She modified her tone so as not to appear as rude as her words indicated.

"Sorry."

"No, I'm sorry. It's just . . . I'm sick of people prying into my affairs." She grabbed a roll and broke it open.

"Prying into your affairs and being genuinely interested in helping are two different things."

"Coming from a total stranger, it's prying, believe me." Stella flashed him a brittle smile. She buttered the roll with excessive vigor. Fresh homemade bread, it smelled delicious. She hadn't eaten real butter for years.

"Look . . ." The professional star surfaced momentarily. "You're all very kind, you and Leo and your family. I really do thank you for helping me out tonight. But I'm on my way somewhere else. I've known you for a matter of hours, and I'll never see you again after tomorrow. You're not really interested in my affairs, and I assure you I'm not interested in yours. Let's just accept that." She gave him her professional, blank smile and went back to her roll.

Jonathan attacked his steak with barely repressed fury. What a stuck-up, patronizing cow! Wait till she finds out she will be staying after all. Selfish, self-centered, spoiled — all words beginning with *S* to go with her name. Stella, Sue, Susanna. Maybe she wasn't the person to wear his clothes after all. Might give off completely the wrong image. Koolwear for the selfish celebrity. Why waste his time with her? He must be mad to think she'd consider getting involved with it.

"Believe me, I'm not the slightest bit interested in your precious affairs," he said.

Stella nibbled at a piece of lettuce. She'd been very rude. Unpardonably so. The silence almost twanged, taut as a string on her guitar. Jonathan was a nice man. A good, decent man. He didn't deserve her prima donna treatment. Who did?

"I'm sorry, that was completely uncalled for." Then, after a pause, with raised eyebrows and a knowing smile, she tossed out, "Doreen says you're engaged."

"Aren't you prying just a little?" The words snapped out. Brittle. Tense.

"Seems common knowledge. Don't you country people know one another's business? Community spirit and all that? Being engaged is hardly something you'd want to keep secret."

"I'm not engaged, as it happens." Still tight-lipped.

"Really? You'll have to update Doreen." Stella gave him a cheeky little grin and crunched into a carrot stick. "Sorry."

"People make assumptions."

"They do, don't they?"

Her lips twisted in a gesture he recognized from one of the publicity shots he'd seen last time he was in Sydney. Promoting a concert she'd given at the casino in Darling Harbour. It looked provocative and sexy then. Now it made him grind his teeth in anger.

"What do you do for entertainment in a place like this?" she asked next.

"I told you. Karaoke on Saturday nights."

"That's it?"

"We make our own entertainment. We don't have to *be* entertained." He speared a piece of lettuce with a vicious stab of his fork. "We follow our local cricket and football teams if they're playing close to town. There's an outdoor movie theatre at Cooper's Creek."

"Outdoor?"

"Deck chairs. BYO."

"BYO what?"

"Everything."

"Except, presumably, the movie."

Jonathan looked at her sharply. Stella ate potato salad and waited innocently for his reply. She was enjoying herself all of a sudden, keeping this man off balance. He was so irritatingly sure of himself, it must be a new sensation for him to be laughed at. Especially by a woman. By the look of the competition, Jonathan Knight would be the most eligible bachelor for hundreds of kilometers in any direction.

"I've never been to an outdoor movie." She hadn't been to a movie in public for years. It had become almost impossible unless she wore a disguise and sneaked in, in the dark. No fun at all.

"Well, you wouldn't have, would you?"

"Why not?" Alert and suspicious all of a sudden.

"Coming from the city."

"How do you know I come from the city?"

"It's obvious," he countered. "You look as if you do. You act as if you do. You dress as if you do."

"Yes, now. But I could have been born anywhere."

Jonathan studied her. He knew she'd been born in Sydney's southern beach suburb Cronulla. It was on the liner notes of one of the CDs.

"True," he said.

"Where were you born?"

"Here."

"In the pub?" Now she really did laugh, a deep-throated, gurgling chuckle that forced a smile in response.

He met her sparkling eyes. "No, smarty-pants. In Koologong. Mum couldn't get to the hospital in time, so Dad delivered me at home."

"Wow. Where, exactly, do you live? Not in one of those, um, houses down the street?"

"No. Out of town. Fifteen kilometers east. The turnoff's near the factory. Jingaluck is right on the river in a little valley."

"Hard to imagine a river out here."

"There are several, actually. Cotton farmers need a reliable source to irrigate the crop. Our river rarely runs dry."

"Lucky."

He nodded with open enthusiasm. "Yes. Water is always the biggest problem. Getting a regular supply and the right amount constantly flowing to the crop. We've been studying it in detail, and there are some really interesting results from other farms. . . ." He stopped, aware he'd begun a lecture on water management and that most people weren't the slightest bit interested, least of all a woman like this one. "Sorry. It's pretty boring, I know."

Stella shook her head. "Other people's passions often are. I met someone once who told me in great depth about his collection of World War One model airplanes. Never occurred to him I might not be as enthusiastic as he was." It happened to her all the time, people telling her things, expecting to enthrall her, thinking they knew her. She had always been very polite, listened, asked questions, and smiled.

"Sorry."

She smiled. "Don't be. It's important to you, and you should be passionate about it. Doreen says the whole town is depending on this factory of yours."

"Yes."

"Big responsibility. Why have you taken it on?" She really did want to know and wasn't just making conversation.

He thought for a moment. "I didn't set out to be the town savior. It just seemed to happen. Keith and I worked our guts out and didn't get anywhere with sheep or cattle. We had to come up with some other approach. Purely selfish reasons." His mouth curved into a smile.

A little tingle of attraction fluttered somewhere. Stella picked up the last slice of cucumber. Jonathan continued. As he spoke, the magnitude of the task he'd inadvertently undertaken became more and more apparent.

"I decided we should try cotton. Did you know that Australia is one of the top exporters? After a few years of hard work it seemed to make good business sense to cut out the middle man, which is where the town came in. We're a cooperative style company, despite what they tell you. We send the raw product out to be spun and woven at the nearest mill, but it comes straight back to Koologong to be sewn. We've sent a few youngsters off to technical college on the strength of the factory's offering them employment when they qualify. Not just as seamstresses, but in agriculture as well."

"Who designs your clothes? Surely you don't do that too?" Stella smiled. He really was beginning to sound like Superman. He had every reason to be proud, whether he realized he was or not.

"A woman I met at university, Lena Worrell."

"The fiancée?" The smile widened.

"The not fiancée, although we did consider marriage once," said Jonathan, not smiling back. "Lena is a city girl through and through. She hates it out here."

The way he said it, plus the scowl, made it clear that he thought Lena was at fault.

"What have you got against us city girls? I detect a real bias, Mr. Knight."

"What have I got against city girls? Let me see. Let's try shallow, greedy, hard, callous, selfish, superficial, wanting instant solutions to things, easily bored, image conscious, status conscious, impatient . . ."

"I think you're repeating yourself," said Stella mildly as he paused for breath. "You are joking, of course?" Lena must be some piece of work to instigate this diatribe!

"Am I?"

"Nobody could generalize so wildly and expect to be taken seriously."

"Maybe I am just a bit," he admitted. "I

had enough of city life when I was at university in Sydney. It's all too fast and too uncaring, too noisy and polluted for me. I couldn't wait to get back out here." He gave her a studied look. "I s'pose that makes me a hick from the bush."

She smiled into his eyes. "Yes. And I'm a shallow, callous city girl who just can't wait to get back to the noise and the pollution. But I don't think I'm half the things you accuse me and my city sisters of."

He dropped his gaze to his empty plate. She was right, of course, but bitterness over Lena's long-running distaste for the bush and disappointment over her recent defection from Koolwear lent acid to his tongue. And judging by the edge in Stella's voice despite the smile on her face, she was a long way from becoming the Koolwear girl. Time for a change of topic — and fast.

"No. I'm sure you're not." He smiled what he hoped was an engaging smile. "How about a swim later? It's great at night. The water's cool, and you've never seen so many stars as out here. Not in the city. Full moon tonight too."

Stella blinked as her mind switched gears. Plunge her whole body into a pool of cool, refreshing water? Swimming with Jonathan? "Sounds wonderful."

"Shall we go? We can have coffee at home."

He drove out of town on the road Stella had come in on. She studied his profile. He turned his head suddenly, a small crease in his brow giving him a slightly anxious look.

"I won't molest you or in any way harass you," he said.

"If I thought for one minute you would, I'd never consider your offer. Anyway, I've done self-defense training. I can break your arm and disable you before you even know what's hit you."

"Really?"

Stella nodded and kept a straight face as he stared at her in astonishment before returning his attention to the road. She could do it too. Xavier and Julianne had insisted she be able to defend herself, if necessary. She couldn't imagine having to lay a hand on Jonathan in anger. She'd much prefer to touch him in more intimate and gentle ways.

The thought surprised her. She'd temporarily given up on men, put ideas of love and closeness out of her mind. Mark had soured her view of his gender pretty effectively, and in her business, relationships were too fraught with publicity and gossip.

And too many eager guys were only too willing to trade on her reputation for their own benefit. They came fitted with ulterior motives. But this man — to him she was an ordinary girl, and an ordinary girl could enjoy herself. If she pleased.

Her eyes kept straying to his tanned thighs in khaki shorts on the seat beside her. The short sleeves of his cotton shirt displayed muscled arms. The hands gripping the steering wheel were strong. Working hands. The male hands she'd experienced had always been as soft and well manicured as her own. These were strong, tough hands that took what they wanted with confidence and certainty. What would they feel like running over her skin? She already knew. He'd lifted her as if she were a child.

She wondered what Mr. Mover and Shaker would say if he knew who she was and what images had passed through her mind. A soft chuckle erupted from somewhere deep inside her.

He looked across at her, eyes narrowed, smile hovering. "What's funny?"

"Nothing, nothing." The chuckle turned into a laugh.

"I'm glad I amuse you."

His voice was so cool, Stella stifled her giggles. "I'm sorry. I'm not laughing at you.

It's just that this whole situation is so ridiculous. I have plenty of money, but I can't access it, and here I am, forced to accept a bed from a stranger. Koologong was just a spot on the map I was passing through. It's crazy."

"It's fate. You were meant to stop here." He gave her a little sidelong smile.

"Why would that be?" Stella smiled back.

"Who knows? It's fate. It just happens. Serendipity."

"Hmm." Stella screwed up her nose. "Isn't 'serendipity' a lucky accident?"

"Right."

"Not so lucky from where I'm sitting. Apart from meeting you, that is," she added hastily.

"I rest my case." Jonathan laughed.

"My meeting you or the other way around?" She laughed as well.

"Remains to be seen. Could be mutually beneficial."

Her laughter faded. "I can't imagine I have anything to offer you in return for your helping me this way."

Stella stared out the side window. The golden orb of the sun hovered low on the far horizon, sending purple and rose red light flooding across the sky. A magnificent outback sunset. She'd become accustomed to the openness of the landscape and the vastness of the sky, but the sunsets still took her breath away.

"I want to get on the road tomorrow. Do you think Dan will have finished fixing my car?"

"I don't know whether 'finished' is the appropriate term. Accurate, maybe."

"Pardon?" Stella tilted her head, not sure she'd heard correctly over the roar of the engine.

"I don't know," he said in a clear, loud voice. "That sort of little car is better suited for the city."

She smiled. "Should I be driving a pickup like yours?"

He grinned. " 'Pickup'? You've been in the States too long. It's a 'ute,' remember?"

"A 'ute.' Of course it is." She sighed. "There are so many of those language differences, I forget what belongs where. Takes me ages to switch my head over from one country to the other — lifts and elevators, torches and flashlights, cantaloupes and rockmelons, ground floors and first floors. That one confused me for ages."

"Well, we're pretty ordinary in Koologong. Fair dinkum Aussies." He laughed.

She laughed as well. "Does anyone actually say 'fair dinkum' anymore?"

77

"Yeah. Grandpa does." He paused. "Would you like to see the factory before you leave? You'll probably have the morning here, and there's not much to do. We're air-conditioned."

"Air-conditioning that works?" Stella narrowed her eyes.

"Absolutely! My workers would revolt otherwise."

"It's a date!"

"The air-conditioning does it every time." He sent her a rueful glance, and she laughed.

He slowed for a left turn onto a dusty dirt side road. Tree-dotted paddocks stretched away on both sides.

"Look!" cried Stella. A mob of kangaroos camouflaged among the tree trunks lifted their heads, ears twitching, poised for flight. Two stood very close to the roadside.

Jonathan slowed to a crawl. "Mad things," he said. "Never know where they're going to go." As if to prove his point, first one and then the other leaped directly in front of the vehicle, cleared the fence with ease, and joined the mob bounding away into the gathering gloom.

Ten minutes later the ute topped a rise. "Home," he announced.

Emphasized by the softness of the evening

light, Jingaluck glowed like an oasis of green in the predominantly brown landscape, nestled in the river valley a few hundred meters from a winding stream whose path was delineated by gums and wattle. They turned through a gate, which she opened and closed, splashed across a shallow ford, passed briefly through a stand of pine trees, then bounced up the long driveway to the house. Tall gums and more pines shaded it from the worst of the heat, and a covered veranda ran the length of the front and disappeared down both sides. Several cane chairs and a swinging seat beckoned invitingly. The lawn, which must have been carefully tended at some stage, had been left to fend for itself, although it wore a tinge of green. Thanks to recent rain, Jonathan said when she commented.

Roses were in full bloom along the edge of the veranda. Bright patches of red and pink from geraniums in pots on the steps leading to the house lent a welcoming, cheerful air. Jingaluck looked like a home. A well-loved, comfortable home.

As they got out, a black dog emerged from under the veranda and ran to Jonathan, wiggling its whole body along with its wagging tail. Jon gave the dog's back a slap of greeting. Clouds of dust billowed out. "This is

Lancelot."

"Lancelot?"

Furry ears pricked up at his name.

"One of the knights," explained Jonathan.

The dog sniffed her legs. She patted his head gingerly. A nose-wrinkling odor permeated the air around him, along with a cloud of flies. He'd been rolling in something unpleasant or long dead. Not the most courtly behavior.

"Are there more?" She stepped away toward the house.

"No. We had Galahad, but a snake bit him. King Arthur died of old age last year. There are a couple of cats about the place."

"Oh, dear." Stella glanced at him, but he didn't seem particularly perturbed about the dogs.

"Come in." Jonathan led her through the small white gate to the house yard, along a stone pathway bisecting the struggling lawn, and up several wooden steps to the veranda.

"The roses are lovely." She stopped to sniff deeply from a beautiful yellow bloom in the hope of removing Lancelot's pong from her nose.

"Renata saved every spare drop she could to keep them going through the worst of the drought. Can't let everything die."

"But you've got a swimming pool."

"A luxury. We've only just refilled it with bore water. It was empty for three years. Handy if a bushfire comes through."

"Gosh! Is that likely?" *Drought, fire, oppressive heat?* What else was there to contend with?

"It's always a possibility in summer."

Jonathan pulled open the screen door, sweeping an arm wide to allow her precedence.

Stella stepped inside and gave a spontaneous cry of delight. "It's so cool!"

"Yes. Stays that way pretty much."

She stood in a wide entry foyer. A hallway with the same polished wood floor led to the back of the house. To the right through a broad archway was a spacious living room with two comfortable-looking sofas and a couple of easy chairs grouped around a low coffee table. A TV sat in a corner but didn't appear to be the central feature of the room. An old upright piano with a vase of roses on top, a stereo system, and bookshelves crammed with CDs and books ran along one wall. She'd investigate those later.

"Hello. Welcome, Sue." The woman had an unmistakable Dutch accent. "I am Renata." She also had short, wispy blond hair, a round, smiling face, twinkling blue eyes, and she was hurrying from the depths of the house with outstretched arms, delivering a firm kiss, European style, on both cheeks.

"Sue Starkey. Thank you very much for letting me crash in on you like this." She glanced at Jonathan and smiled. "It's very kind."

"No problem. We have plenty of room. Come. I'll show you. And that noodle-head Dan locked up your suitcase? Pah!" Stella flung a grin over her shoulder at Jonathan as Renata bustled away down the corridor, still talking. "Never mind. I have spare clothes. Come." She flung a door open.

"What a lovely room." Stella stopped in the doorway. She didn't know what she'd expected, but it wasn't this. A woman's room decorated in delicate cream and pink rosebud wallpaper, the bed covered with a white lace spread over a deep rose-colored duvet. An antique oak dressing table with a large oval swing mirror, elaborate brass handles on the drawers, and two small cut-crystal trays with nothing in them, sitting on the top. Heavy cream curtains were pulled closed against the heat of the day. More polished wood flooring, but here, a shaggy Flokati rug lay by the bed.

"Yes, I put you in Caroline's room."

"Caroline?" Doreen had mentioned a Caroline. An aunt? The way Doreen relayed information, Caroline could equally easily be Jonathan's daughter or grandmother.

"Keith and Jon's little sister. She's . . . away. Prefers the city." A frown passed across Renata's cheery face, for a moment eclipsing the smile. "She's a troubled soul. Poor girl. They haven't seen her in years."

"Jonathan didn't mention his sister." Stella walked to the bed. Renata had left a folded towel along with a new toothbrush in its packet lying on the chair by the dressing table. "Thank you very much for this. Would it be all right to have a shower?"

"Of course. I hung a couple of blouses and a dress in the cupboard there. All Kool-wear." Her smile revealed strong white teeth. "Maybe a little big on you but not much." She ran a critical eye up and down Stella's decidedly hot and grimy body.

"You're very kind. I don't know how I can ever repay you."

Renata waved a hand airily. "No need. The bathroom is across the way. Use whatever you need, cosmetics and so on. We'll be out back by the pool. Follow your nose." She pointed to the rear of the house. "Oh, by the way, don't drink the water. We always have a jug of boiled water in the fridge for drinking."

■ ■ ■ ■

Jonathan relaxed into a recliner with a sigh. "Well, I got her here."

The stifling heat had gone from the evening, chased away by a breeze that rustled the leaves of the peppercorns and gums overhead. Soft darkness met the glow from the house lights at the edge of the paved terrace. The water in the pool reflected silver ripples a few meters away. Would Stella still like to swim tonight?

"I don't want anything to do with this, Jonno. You're playing with fire." Keith crossed his legs and folded his arms behind his head, staring up into the night sky.

Jonathan squashed his guilt and qualms about the whole operation beneath defiant indignation. "I'm not forcing her into anything. She genuinely needed help, so I offered. She accepted of her own free will. If Dan hadn't locked her bag up, she'd be in the hotel tonight."

Keith shook his head, wearing his stubborn face. "It doesn't feel right."

Jonathan sighed. It didn't feel right anymore. It had in the pub when he first laid eyes on her, before he actually spoke to her. Before she became a real person. But now . . . well, he needn't follow up. He wouldn't. Let her be. Let the whole thing slide away. She need never know.

"You won't say anything, will you? She obviously doesn't want anyone to know who she is. It really would upset her. Just play along the way she wants. She's Sue from the city stuck here while her car's being fixed. End of story."

"Maybe she is." Keith chuckled. "Better go and check out your CD covers. You've got all of them, haven't you? Everything she's done?"

"Cripes." Jonathan sprang to his feet. "I'd better go and take them off the shelf, in case she sees them." How would he explain? Would such a big fan not recognize her? She'd never believe him.

"Still got that crush on her?"

"Shut up, Keith. She might hear you."

"No, she won't." Renata put a tray with mugs of coffee on the outdoor table. "She's taking a shower." She sat down next to Keith and lifted her feet onto his lap. "Lovely girl. Are you sure she's Stella Starr?"

"I'll put the CDs on your bed so you can check for yourself. See what you think. But whatever you do, don't let her see them, and don't say anything." Jonathan strode to the back door and, out of sight of the others, almost ran to the living room. The shower was clearly audible as he passed the bathroom. He'd definitely hear her come out.

How many CDs were there? Not eleven years' worth. Contrary to Keith's crack, he didn't have them all. He had her first three and the latest two. He whipped them off the shelf and shuffled others along to fill the gap. *Right.* Into Keith and Renata's bedroom with them.

Their room was at the far end of the rambling house, in the wing Granddad had added years ago with their own sitting room. It wasn't used much, but it ensured everyone had their privacy. Jonathan sat on their bed and studied each CD in turn.

The first one, titled *Stella,* was the career launcher. A massive hit when she was only fifteen. She'd been big for about two years; then the spotlight dimmed and moved on to dazzle someone else. She evolved into a steady performer with a solid fan base of people like himself. No hits anywhere near as big as the first album, but always there. Everyone had heard of her. Australians, according to the media, regarded her as their own. The pretty, shy, talented schoolgirl plucked from nowhere and dropped into everyone's life.

If she did something noteworthy, like get married or divorced, her picture made the front page, or close to. These photos, the early teenage ones, weren't much use. Eleven years was a long time in the entertainment world.

The most recent CD he had, released last year, showed her in profile at the piano — a distance shot. Her hair was long and light brown, honey-colored, hanging like a curtain, obscuring her face as she played. Useless. The liner notes provided even less information.

He stacked the discs on the bed and left, closing the door and making sure it latched. The bathroom door was open and Caroline's room door closed. What would Stella think of the clothes? He'd asked Renata to give her a choice of as many garments as she could rustle up so she would get an idea of the range available, the colors and feel of the fabric. Pity that Renata wasn't the same size, but they were close enough.

He clenched his fists and grimaced. Maybe she'd like Koolwear all on her own, suggest later herself that she wear it. *Fat chance.* She'd forget about the people and the clothes as soon as she hit the road.

■ ■ ■ ■

The dress was too big. Stella peered at herself in the swing mirror from several angles before deciding she couldn't get away with such gaping armholes. Nice style, though. Lena was talented. Perhaps tomorrow at the factory . . . if they had it in white.

Have to put her shorts back on. She scanned the blouses one by one, discarding the long-sleeved blue as too hot and the white as too big, buttoning too low to wear comfortably, especially in front of Jonathan and his brother. She slipped on a lovely sea green sleeveless shirt, loosely knotting the trailing ends over her stomach. Not a bad fit. Soft, silky fabric with a polished finish. Comfortable, stylish, and cool.

She smiled at her now clean, refreshed reflection and did a happy little dance step. She was so lucky to have taken up Jonathan's offer. Serendipity indeed. The pub wouldn't have been anywhere near as nice as this. And Renata was a sweetie. What about Keith? Another Knight in shining armor? She laughed softly. Jonathan was. He'd saved her, even if his armor was a pair of khaki shorts, work boots, a well-washed blue shirt, and an Akubra hat.

She fluffed her rapidly drying hair with both hands. It felt wonderfully cool on her scalp. A yawn escaped suddenly. Maybe she'd have a swim in the morning. Jonathan would understand.

Stella opened the door and headed for the rear of the house, where Renata had told her they would be, outside by the pool enjoying the evening. She followed the sound of voices, a burst of male laughter. The screen door banged behind her as she stepped onto the veranda. Three steps led down to a paved area surrounding the in-ground pool. The temperature had dropped. A soft breeze washed over her skin and lifted the damp hair on her neck.

"Feeling better?" Jonathan rose to greet her.

"Yes, thanks," she murmured. Stella stopped, smiling uncertainly as the other man looked her up and down with appraising eyes. Did he mind having a total stranger in his house?

"G'day." He lumbered to his feet and stuck out his hand. "Keith Knight."

She grasped his large paw and hung on as he shook hands briskly. A bigger, older, weather-beaten version of Jonathan. Squarer face, more rugged features, more leathery skin, ginger tint to the hair. An outdoors man, a farmer; Jonathan presumably spent more of his time indoors.

"Thanks for letting me stay," she said.

"No worries. Stay as long as you like." He resumed his seat on a recliner.

"Sit down, Sue," said Renata. "The coffee's cold, but I'll make some more."

"Please don't bother. I think I'll go to bed soon. I'm exhausted. It's been a long day." Stella sat on the closest chair.

"How far've you come?" asked Keith.

"From the coast."

"Long drive."

"Yes." She leaned back, drawing in a deep, cleansing breath of the fresh night air. "It's lovely out here. Cooler too."

"We like it." Jonathan sounded pleased at her compliment.

Stella turned to Renata. "Thanks for the clothes and things. The dress was a little too big, unfortunately, but I like this shirt. It's very soft."

"The color suits you." Renata smiled and glanced at Jonathan.

"It does." He spoke quickly. "We use a special technique to get the texture of the fabric right."

Of course! Koolwear. His pride and joy. Not just his, but of all three of them. "I'd like to get one for myself tomorrow. Maybe a dress too." It was the least she could do. He seemed so eager she visit the factory.

"Great. I can take you over in the morning, then drop into town and see what Dan's discovered about your car. Back here for lunch."

"We're heading for Canberra tomorrow remember, Jon." Renata smiled at Stella. "A friend is getting married on Saturday. I'm matron of honor."

"How lovely."

"Maybe you'd like to go in my place," suggested Keith. "Weddings are for women."

"Weren't you involved in Renata's?" asked Jonathan. "I thought I saw you there."

"Ours was small. This one's turning into a monster. I always quite liked Maria, but she's gone crazy."

"I know what you mean," murmured Stella with a grimace. Hers had been a three-ring circus. It took on a life of its own completely beyond her control, stage-managed by Xavier and Mark's PR system. The bride and groom were the last to have a say.

"Are you married?" asked Renata.

"I was. I'm not now."

"You can't have been married very long. You're too young."

"Keith!" cried Renata. "Don't be so nosy."

"Three years," replied Stella. "It was a disaster. We never should have done it. *I* never should have done it." She sighed. "But it's over now."

Renata pulled a commiserating face. "It's always sad when marriages don't work out."

"You have to be careful whom you marry in the first place," said Jonathan. "Wait for the right person."

"There speaks the expert," scoffed Keith. "If you wait too long, you'll be too old to enjoy it."

Stella yawned so widely, her eyes watered. And again. "I'm sorry. I'll have to go to bed, or I'll fall asleep right here." She stood up. The others rose as well.

"We'll be gone by seven, so we may not see you." Renata kissed Stella again on both cheeks. "We're taking a few extra days and having a little break. Back on Wednesday. First holiday in three years."

Keith shook her hand. "Nice to meet you, Sue."

"Good night and good-bye, just in case. Thank you once more."

Jonathan said, "I'll see you in the morning. Leave about nine?" He smiled.

"Fine. I'll try to get up early enough for a swim." She turned and headed for her deliciously inviting bed.

"She's a very nice girl," said Renata when the screen door had closed.

"Are you positive she's Stella Starr? She's nothing like I imagined she'd be." Keith looked from Jonathan to Renata and back to Jonathan.

Jonathan stared after her. She was a nice girl. Not what he'd originally thought at all. She wasn't a stuck-up city miss, hadn't complained, had a tantrum, or made demands on anyone, wore Renata's clothes with a smile, and was genuinely short of money. There was also the surprising vulnerability and lack of confidence.

Could he have made a mistake? What if this girl wasn't Stella Starr but plain, ordinary Sue Starkey as she said she was? A woman who simply bore a striking resemblance and the same surname and first initial. What then? What sort of idiot would he look when everyone found out?

CHAPTER FOUR

Dawn light creeping through the curtains woke Stella. She lay with a pale pink sheet draped across her body, staring at the old-fashioned molded cornices on the ceiling and following paths between the faded rosebuds on the wallpaper as the light grew stronger.

There'd been similar wallpaper in her room as a child. The memory filtered in along with other images. Life had been simple then. She'd gone to school, played with her friends, eaten her meals, done her homework, daydreamed, gone to her piano lessons, practiced, sang. Always sang. Before Dad died and Mum began her decline into another secret world. Before Xavier heard her sing in a high school musical and shoved her into the glare of the spotlight from which she had never escaped. Until now.

Stella turned over, crumpling the sheet in uncomfortable bunches beneath her hip.

She tugged and straightened, then lay still. Running away didn't solve anything. It only gave her a respite. She'd have to go back eventually. Apart from all the other positives and negatives of her life, she genuinely loved what she did. Singing and entertaining people. But after the humiliation and crushing defeat of her marriage, the time had come to examine who Stella Starkey really was. Not Xavier's Stella Starr. She knew *her;* she only had to pick up a magazine to find out about Stella Starr. No, she wanted to discover the Stella who'd been stunted at fifteen.

That Stella, alias Sue, wasn't doing terribly well at the moment, she had to admit. If her car wasn't repaired today, she'd be forced to ask Jonathan Knight for a bed for the weekend. She had precisely twenty-nine dollars and thirty-five cents left.

Give up? Admit defeat? She could ring Xavier. He'd charter a plane, and she'd be home by this afternoon. He'd organize the media; there'd be photographers and TV reporters and oozing interviewers pretending to care but hoping she'd do or say something hysterical and crazy. All that would happen when she went home anyway.

But she wasn't ready yet. Her mouth firmed, and she reached to pick up her watch from the bedside table. Seven-fifteen. Much later than she expected. Renata and Keith would be long gone, and it'd be warming up outside already. She'd loosen up stiff joints with a run through her martial arts routines. Afterward a swim would be perfect, then breakfast and the factory trip.

She sat up, yawned, stretched, and slipped on the green shirt to head for the bathroom. What a warm, close family, so confident in their love for one another. So welcoming. Had her family ever been like that? She couldn't remember.

Jonathan. What a strange man he was. Annoyingly obsequious at first, hovering around being helpful, making her suspicious and snappy, but then he'd genuinely charmed her at dinner. Perhaps her initial opinion had been colored by her own circumstances, the annoyance and worry at being stuck out here alone in the heat, surrounded by strangers. She'd never been totally alone before. Someone else had always organized things for her, told her what to do. Like a child.

Across the table, with just the two of them, she'd caught a glimpse of the real Jonathan Knight. The one who inspired and harangued the townspeople into supporting his cotton venture. The man with intelligence, vision, and determination and a deep love for the country and the place he was born. He wanted to preserve his property and his inheritance, but with it he wanted to save the town from drying up and blowing away with the red dust on the land. He'd fight hard for what he wanted.

Stella had driven through several small settlements like Koologong on her relatively aimless journey. One man had told her, as she paid for her petrol, that the banks had begun closing their country branches. When that happened, the local shops died, because people went to the bigger centers to bank and naturally did their shopping there. She'd had no idea of the problems people faced out here. She never read newspapers beyond the entertainment pages and rarely watched TV news. She wasn't even in Australia for months at a time. Now, with her blasé and, as it turned out, naïve assumption that everyone took credit cards, she was virtually penniless. And stranded.

If her Sir Jonathan hadn't appeared, where would she be? Stella grinned at herself in the mirror as she combed her hair and secured it in a ponytail.

What would be appropriate swimwear?

Jonathan walked slowly toward the house

with a bucket of newly collected eggs, his eyes fixed on the figure in the shade by the pool. She was practicing some sort of martial arts, punching and kicking in a rhythmical, powerful sequence. No wonder she told him she could break his arm. She released the strikes like a whiplash. Who'd have guessed such a slim body could pack such a wallop?

Was this girl Stella or Sue? The question had twisted his brain most of the night. She was very fit. Stella Starr had a similar build, but he had no idea if she was a martial arts devotee. She'd danced as part of her early stage shows but stopped as she grew older. Nowadays she concentrated on the music, wrote her own songs, sang and played guitar or piano, solo or with a band. If he could get her to sing, there'd be no doubt.

She stopped and wiped her face with her hands, walked about shaking her arms to loosen them. Next came deep-breathing exercises, raising and lowering her arms with hypnotic slowness, totally focused. Jonathan moved on his way. How to get her to sing . . .

He entered the house quietly so as not to disturb her concentration. Fresh eggs for breakfast if she liked. He stowed the eggs in the pantry, filling the jug to make tea when she came in. She was just visible through the kitchen window. Lancelot lay close by under a tree watching her with great interest, red tongue lolling.

Ten minutes later the screen door banged. Jonathan looked up from yesterday's newspaper as she came into the kitchen, face flushed, body slick with sweat.

"Hi," she said with a brilliant smile. "Whew. It's hot already."

Dazzled by the radiance, the closeness, and the sudden, intense conviction that this really was Stella Starr, he managed to come up with, "Supposed to be hotter today than yesterday," in a hoarse voice. He cleared his throat. "Sleep well?"

"Oh, yes! Marvelous, thanks. I was exhausted. I hope Keith and Renata didn't mind that I went to bed so early. I hope I wasn't rude."

"No, they understood. None of us stay up late. Are you ready for breakfast?"

"I am, but I thought I'd have a quick swim first, if it's all right."

"Fine. No hurry."

"Hmm." She paused, biting her lower lip gently. "Renata didn't mention a swimming costume I could use, did she?"

Jonathan smiled. "Not keen on skinny-dipping?"

Her eyes widened. "No, not since I was about three. And certainly not with you hovering around."

He laughed. "Thought so. Caroline left some stuff. Could be a costume in a drawer somewhere."

"Would she mind?"

He shook his head. "We haven't seen her for years. I'm sure she's bought herself another one by now."

"Great. I'll have a look." Stella stopped in the doorway, smiling. "Are you swimming?"

"No. I've got some papers to sort before we go to the factory. And I'll start breakfast soon."

"Thanks, Jonathan. I . . ." Her green eyes met his. She held the contact for a moment, then looked down. "I'm so grateful," she murmured. "I don't . . ."

"It's fine," he said briskly. "Forget it. Anyone would do the same."

She looked at him again, a slight crease in her smooth brow. "Would they? I wonder."

"Out here? Yes."

The smile reappeared, sunny and bright. "I suppose I'm just not used to people being kind for no other reason than to be helpful. It's refreshing." She laughed. "I'm from the evil city, you see. It's dog-eat-dog where I come from."

Jonathan laughed, but the smile faded as she disappeared down the hallway. Colin and the others were right. He hadn't thought this through properly. She'd be very upset when she discovered his ulterior motive. Extremely upset. He firmed his lips, forehead furrowed in thought. His best hope was that she'd be so impressed by the Koolwear garments and the factory, she'd make a point of wearing their gear in the future. And telling her friends about it as well.

"Could we go into town first, Jonathan? I'd like to pick up my bag and check on the car."

"Sure." He sounded doubtful, almost disappointed. The sun shone in their eyes now, as they left the Jingaluck driveway and turned east for the highway. The huge clear blue bowl of the sky provided no relief from the building heat. Oppressive, the idea of an unstoppable rise in temperature — something to be endured until the relief of nightfall. But complaining wouldn't do any good.

"I don't want to be a nuisance. You can drop me. You don't need to stay."

He glanced at his watch as he drove. "I should get to work. I have some things to do, but I can be back by about eleven."

"With any luck, I'll be able to drive myself to the factory." And then away to somewhere cooler and greener. Forget Lightning Ridge; she'd head northeast for the coast or maybe south, following Keith and Renata.

"Hmm." He slowed at the intersection for the highway. Dust from their wheels caught up and swirled around the ute in a fine reddish cloud. A double-length cattle truck thundered by, heading for Koologong and beyond. Jonathan swung in behind it.

The little collection of buildings hunkered down against another searing day. Nothing stirred in the broad central street. He dropped her outside the low, corrugated-iron and weatherboard garage building.

"Thanks." She bent to look back in through the open car door, swatting at a fly automatically.

"Wait for me in the pub at about eleven."

"Okay. If I don't see you out there first." She shut the door. He waved and accelerated away.

Stella studied the garage. It didn't inspire confidence, with paint in a variety of colors and a ramshackle air of neglect, two or three wrecked cars lying forlornly in the yard at the side. Propped against a wall was an array of tires, steering wheels, hubcaps, and other metal items that belonged inside or on vehicles of one sort or another.

But all Dan needed to do was give her enough steam to reach the next good-sized town, a hundred or so kilometers away.

The white car that was there yesterday when she left her Ford and which she assumed was Dan's stood in the shade at the front. The padlocked door was open; hammering came from inside.

Stella stepped into the workshop. Her car hung suspended on the hoist. Dan was standing by a bench with a hammer and a piece of metal. He belted vigorously at one end of it, then held it up and examined it with a critical eye. Was that from her car? It looked like a drainpipe.

"Good morning," said Stella.

Dan spun around. The hammer dropped with a crash to the concrete floor. He leaped aside as it bounced near his foot.

"Crikey, you gave me a fright!"

"Sorry. How are you getting on with my car?"

From Dan's expression, she could be speaking a foreign language. She gestured toward the hoist. His gaze followed where she pointed, and he did a comical double take.

"Oh, yeah!"

She waited. Dan bent down and picked

up the hammer.

"Well?"

"What?"

"What's the matter?"

"Nuthin'."

Stella frowned. He couldn't possibly be right. "Nothing's wrong with the car? Why was it coughing and losing power?"

"Oh, the car! I thought you meant me." Dan chuckled. "Nuthin's wrong with me!"

Stella let that one pass. "Have you discovered what's wrong with my car?" she asked slowly and clearly.

"It's losin' power." Stella opened her mouth, but Dan continued. "Fuel's not gettin' through properly." Now they were getting somewhere.

"Can you fix it?"

"Dunno."

"Would I be able to get to the next town? Say, Walgett?"

"Maybe. Maybe not." He shrugged.

Stella resisted the urge to grab the hammer and hit him on the head with it.

"Wouldn't want to break down out there on the road somewhere."

Then she could wrap the drainpipe around his neck.

"No." She took a deep, calming breath. "When do you think you'll know what's wrong?"

He screwed up his face in deep thought. "Next week sometime? Might have to get some parts in. That takes time. Hard to say exactly how long."

"Next week!"

"Might not be that quick. Wouldn't count on it."

Stella knew when she was beaten. "May I have my suitcase, please? It's in the car."

He grinned. "Yeah, no worries." He pressed a red button to lower the hoist.

She took her bag from the back seat and slammed the door with a very satisfying bang. Dan went back to his drainpipe. She struggled out the door and across the road with her red case bouncing behind her on little wheels designed to roll on smooth airport tiles and carpeted hotel hallways, not rough bitumen and soft red dust.

When she reached the hotel, she shoved the door open with one hip and dragged the case inside. Leo was fiddling about behind the bar. He straightened up when she barged in.

"Hello, love." His surprise was undeniable. "Everything go all right out at Jingaluck?"

"Hello, Leo. Yes, no problem. Jonathan just dropped me off. Could I please use the ladies room to change? I finally rescued my suitcase."

His concerned expression relaxed to the usual good cheer. "Use the room upstairs."

"No, no, I couldn't — the ladies room will be fine, thanks."

The suitcase bumped against chairs and occasionally slewed sideways into a wall, but Stella didn't care if it went right through and put a hole in Leo's aging, battered plaster work. She'd had enough of this place — the heat, the flies, the dust, the constant roar of cicadas, Dan and his hopeless "don't care" attitude. She laid the dusty case on the floor of the washroom and dug out fresh clothes and her other sandals with flat heels. If she kept herself occupied, the rest of her simmering anger wouldn't erupt and create a volcanic mess.

She stripped off Renata's green shirt and her dirty shorts with grim determination, swapping them for a blue striped singlet-style dress. Four or five more days? Impossible — no money, stifling heat, a sick car, a mechanic with no discernible brain. Country-style kindness would have its limits. No way could she ask the Knights for another week's accommodation.

She wielded her hairbrush in short, sharp strokes, staring with a grim, set mouth at her reflection in the yellowing mirror. What to do? Throw herself on the mercy of Leo? See if he had a solution? She returned to the bar.

"Leo, I have a problem." He smiled with eyebrows raised politely. Stella paused. How best to ask? Straight out, probably. "Dan says my car won't be fixed until next week. He doesn't seem to know." Dan was an idiot, pure and simple.

"The problem being?" prompted Leo.

"I don't have much cash, and I can't afford to pay you for more than one night — not even one, really." She held her breath. Leo had a kind face. He might let her stay on credit until she could get to Walgett and a cash machine. "I can't ask to stay with the Knights for a whole week. I don't know what to do." To her horror, her voice broke on the last words.

"Gosh, Sue. I'd love to help," he started to say, but he was interrupted by another voice behind her saying, "You can stay at my place. I've already told you." He sounded disappointed, hurt.

Stella closed her eyes and drew a deep breath. He wasn't supposed to be back until eleven. What was he doing? Checking up on her as if she were a child incapable of organizing itself? Expecting her to need further assistance? Irritation coupled with her residual anger at this whole situation, at putting herself in his debt, at appearing silly and weak and incompetent when he was a man she wanted to impress, made her spine stiffen.

"Hello. I didn't expect you for at least half an hour." She gave him her brightest and best smile. "You could do me a favor and take me to Walgett to a bank, and then I won't need to. I don't want to be a nuisance. I hate imposing." Maybe he'd do it if he was so keen to be helpful.

"You won't be." Jonathan returned the smile. "Renata would be furious if she heard I'd forced you to stay at the hotel instead of at Jingaluck."

"Much as I hate to agree with him, Jon's right," said Leo. "That woman is not to be crossed." If she hadn't met Renata, she'd be suspicious of his remark, but as she had . . .

The two men regarded her steadily, Leo grinning happily, Jonathan with a concerned crease in his brow. Stella gave up. Jingaluck was a wonderful place. Infinitely preferable to four or five days in the Central Hotel. "What can I say?"

"Nothing." Jonathan smiled, and all her petty annoyances melted away in the warmth of his expression. *Think positive, enjoy the experience.* She could relax by the pool, read a book from the big collection they had, explore the CDs, and when Jonathan went to work, play the piano. Maybe even write a song.

"Are you sure Dan is a mechanic?" She glanced at Leo, lifting an eyebrow.

Jonathan laughed. "He'll get the job done. Ready? We'll take a run out to the factory for a quick look-see, and then I'll drop you home. I have to go out to one of the fields. Be there the rest of the day. With Keith slacking off, I've got to do his work as well."

No ride to the bank. "Are you sure you want to bother with me? I don't need to see the factory."

"No, no. I promised. Anyway, you'll find it interesting. And cooler." Jonathan grabbed her suitcase and headed for the door.

"Have fun," Leo called.

Stella climbed in beside Jonathan and clicked on her seat belt. Paddocks stretched away into the distance, meeting the blue of the sky in a hazy line that shimmered in the heat. She saw barely a cloud, just the harsh, unrelenting rays of the sun. This was a hard environment. People had to struggle to survive. They grew as tough and rough as the tall gum trees dotting the roadside. No wonder Jonathan was so determined.

Ten kilometers past the Jingaluck road he slowed and turned off to the right on a narrower road. A large sign said *Koolwear* at the intersection.

"Here we are." He pulled the ute into a gravel parking area next to a big shed. All around stretched crops, presumably cotton. *Koolwear* proclaimed the sign on the side of the building above a smaller one saying *Office* next to a blue door.

The tour of inspection took an hour. She'd never seen the inner workings of a manufacturing plant before. Ten workers cutting and sewing, two packing up orders, one in the office manning the phone and the computer. And many more farmers involved out on their properties under the general management of Keith. Jonathan was overseeing and coordinating everything, an amazing achievement.

The two women she'd seen in the pub, introduced as Linda and Alice, eagerly showed her the catalog of clothing and, with Jonathan hovering, Stella chose two dresses, three T-shirts, and two shirts like Renata's, one green, one white. If her small purchases helped these people in some way, all the better. She wielded her credit card.

"Thank goodness you take these." Thank goodness it was in her real surname with just an initial. *S. Starkey* and not *Stella Starr.*

"Can't function without the plastic." Alice swiped the card. Pity Leo didn't feel the same. Linda handed her two paper Kool-wear shopping bags with her clothes.

"Tell your city friends about us," she said. "We could sure do with the publicity."

"I will," promised Stella. "You have a very good product."

"I'd better take you home," said Jonathan. "I have to get out to one of the farms."

When they were retracing their route, he said, "It's no problem, your staying with us, Sue. Make yourself at home. I won't be back until late this evening. Much more comfortable than staying in the pub all day."

"True." Staying at the pub wouldn't have been much fun, chatting with Grandpa while evading his groping hand, or sitting on a bar stool counting the customers. "Shall I cook dinner for you?"

"Can you cook?"

"Of course. What do you think I am?"

"Sorry. City girls, you know? Heat and serve? Microwaves?"

"Not this city girl," said Stella. "I like to cook."

He glanced at her curiously, a question forming, some sort of puzzlement in his expression, but he smiled. "I thought we

111

could have a barbecue."

"Lovely."

"And then a swim."

"Doubly lovely." Stella shifted her bottom on the hot seat. Her dress was sticking to her back. She'd have a swim as soon as he left.

CHAPTER FIVE

Jonathan hurried back to Jingaluck, the setting sun blinding him with golden light. What had Stella been up to all afternoon while he'd been impatiently discussing cotton plants and watering problems and why the crop in Fred Olding's top paddock wasn't doing as well as some of the others? He'd looked at his watch so much, Fred had asked him in his laconic way if he had a train to catch. Then he'd had to sit drinking tea and eating Alma's fruitcake, because a visit there always included a meal, or morning or afternoon tea, plus a good gossip.

His mind was full of her, this outwardly self-possessed woman with the sharp tongue and the brittle manner that hid a vulnerability and softness surprising in such a big star. He'd been fooled by the image. Her stage presence was larger than life. The voice recorded on CDs was strong and vibrant. All the publicity shots and music videos showed a confident, highly talented woman.

Stella, in reality, was sensitive, gentle, smart, in some ways naïve, a little frightened, and a lot out of her depth here in Koologong. Amazing for a woman who spent her life jetting about the world on tour, recording with top-flight musicians, giving sellout concerts, her every whim satisfied.

The old ute bounced and jarred over the potholes as he raced the last few miles to Jingaluck, red dust flying and curling in a plume behind him. He gripped the steering wheel in grimy hands and laughed aloud at the incredible luck of the whole affair.

"Thank you, thank you!" he cried out the open window to whichever god was smiling down upon him from the vast, open skies.

There was absolutely no doubt in his mind whom he had in his house. Preparing his dinner. Sleeping in Caroline's bed. Using his bathroom. Stella Starr, singer extraordinaire. All around gorgeous and beautiful lady, his fantasy girl since the age of seventeen. What had happened to send her off into the wilderness with no money and no support team, no mobile phone and no desire to be rescued by her manager or friends? What problems could a woman like her possibly have?

Whatever they were, they'd be nothing compared to the real ones he and his co-workers and all the people who relied on the Koolwear venture were facing. If the factory went under, Koologong would become a ghost town. Most of the farmers would have to sell out and leave. It was his responsibility to keep them all afloat.

He'd done some investigating on the Internet in his office that morning. The Stella Starr fan Web site had proven very revealing.

According to the message board she'd been spotted shopping in Auckland, swimming at Dunk Island resort, entering a rehab clinic in LA, at the movies in Canberra, boarding a taxi in Perth, and, among other things, was reportedly suffering from a nervous breakdown, cancer, a brain tumor, had had a leg amputated, was recovering from a suicide attempt, or was dead.

In other words, no one had a clue, and her manager was saying nothing. He, one Xavier Perez-Monte, was probably reveling in the attention. It certainly wasn't doing her publicity any harm; because her CD sales had apparently climbed since her disappearance. Could it be a stunt as Alice or Linda had suggested? But she'd be more likely to hole up somewhere with friends in comfort, not drive into the outback alone in the January heat in an anonymous, unreliable little car like the one she was driving.

Renata had studied the photos on his CDs and come to the same conclusion. Susanna was Stella with different hair, clothes, and minimal makeup, but she couldn't hide her figure, and she couldn't change the smile. He'd taken the precaution of hiding said CDs in his underwear drawer. Unless she was a very nosy lady, she wouldn't stumble across them there.

He parked in the garage at the side of the house. Lancelot wandered out to greet him. He paused to pat the grinning black dog.

"How's our guest, eh, fella?" he asked with casual nonchalance in case she happened to be watching out the window, waiting for him to come home. Like a wife. Crikey, talk about a feet-first leap into fantasy-land!

Lancelot wagged his tail and followed him past the pool and the paved barbecue area to the back door, then flopped down in the shade under the veranda. Jonathan pulled off his boots, left them in the laundry, and walked in socks through to the kitchen. A bit like a burglar creeping into his own house. Adrenaline pumped through his body; nerve endings crackled and sparked.

One of his CDs was playing. He cocked his head and listened. The Eagles. He smiled. His heartbeat steadied. There'd always been the slim chance she wouldn't be here, that she'd cracked and called out a recovery team to fly her back to civilization.

Or he'd imagined the whole thing.

"Susanna?"

"Hi." She appeared in the doorway, cool and composed, far happier-looking than this morning. Heartstoppingly beautiful, and she was wearing one of her new Koolwear shirts with a different pair of shorts. Perfect. His heart thumped and jumped. "Like a cold drink?"

"Love one, thanks." He smiled, glad the heat of the day and the red dust could be blamed for his discomfort as much as the sight of her. "I need a shower first, though. I'm filthy and hot."

"You do that, then come and have an appetizer." She gave him one of her brilliant smiles. "On the side veranda. It has a lovely view."

"Appetizer? What have you been up to?"

"Enjoying myself."

The way she spoke, plus her whole manner, implied she didn't enjoy herself very often. As he showered, he thought about it.

He'd always assumed people in her position basically did what they liked, did nothing *but* enjoy themselves. Otherwise, what was the point?

Overlooking the rolling hills, the sweep of the river delineated in the distance by a line of gray-green trees, with the setting sun painting the whole in purple-tinged light, deep in shadow already, the veranda at the side of the house offered his favorite view. Susanna had set the outdoor table with plates, a tall jug of iced juice, and a covered plate of . . . something. A frosty glass stood waiting for him. So did Stella. She fidgeted with the table setting. She couldn't be nervous, could she?

"This looks very pleasant." Jonathan pulled out a chair for her to sit down. Her perfume rose on the warm air and enveloped him like a bouquet. He wanted to let his fingers run across the bare nape of her neck under the ponytail. He wanted to feel the smooth warmth of her body again as he had when he carried her across the road, her breath against his cheek.

He yanked out his own chair and sat opposite her. "What's under the tea towel? I'm starving."

Stella whipped the cloth from the plate to reveal an array of antipasto. She must have improvised with some ingredients, but she'd managed a creditable variety of hors d'oeuvres ranging from olives and salami, through some sort of homemade dip of an odd color with raw vegetables for dipping, to small squares of anchovy toast, slightly burned around the edges.

He lifted his glass. "Cheers." Stella gazed right into his eyes. He couldn't move, under a spell, smitten all over again. His teenage idol. Smiling at him.

"Thank you," she murmured. She lowered her glass.

Jonathan's mind whirled as she plunged deeper and deeper, through his eyes into his very soul. What did she want? Was she giving him some sort of signal? He put his own glass down. Every instinct in his body and every hormone racing in his overheated blood screamed at him to get off his chair and scoop her into his arms. Kiss her and hold her and keep her here forever. Protect her and love her so she never wanted to leave. He shoved his chair back.

"I forgot about the flies!" She flapped and swatted as the little black buzzing hordes descended. "We might have to eat inside after all."

"They are pretty bad." He stood, breathless at being saved from certain humiliation and a possible court appearance for making unwanted advances on a star. "Especially when they smell food. They'll go when it starts getting dark. Then the mozzies come out," he said, attempting a joke through the roaring of blood in his ears.

"I wanted this to be just right." Her mouth drooped forlornly. She dropped the cloth back over the plate and slapped viciously at the flies hovering around her face. "I wanted to do a perfect dinner for you. As a thank you."

Jonathan picked up the plates and cutlery and balanced his glass on top. "You bring the food," he said, and he strode down the veranda to the screen door.

Stella bundled after him, clutching her own glass and the covered platter. *What an idiot.* Any country woman would have known not to try to eat outdoors without tons of fly repellent or in a screened-off area. There were flies in the city but not those tiny little sticky bush flies. They had a persistence all their own. Horrible. Who'd want to live out here? And those deafening cicadas chirping in the gums nonstop from sunup to sundown. And the heat. And the dust.

She followed him to the dining room, cool and dim with its heavy wooden furniture

120

and dark-colored fabrics. She'd only peeked in earlier and stupidly decided against it as too gloomy. He put his cargo on the polished oval table and pulled back curtains. Rosy evening light streamed in, painting shadow patterns on the walls as it passed through the trees.

"I should have thought of this in the first place," she said, placing the platter of appetizers on the table,

"We hardly ever eat in here. Bit formal." Jonathan smiled. "Now. I want my dinner." He lifted the tea towel and grabbed a carrot stick.

"Before you settle down, maybe you should light the barbecue. In case I get that wrong too and blow us up."

"Hey," he said, crunching and swallowing. "Cheer up. So we eat inside. So what? Food's still good. Company's . . ."

" 'Company's . . .'?" Stella looked at him expectantly. What was he going to say? Why the pause?

He rubbed his chin between thumb and forefinger, studying her. "Not bad."

She gave a spontaneous snort of laughter at the seriousness of his expression and the considered nature of the reply. As if he were evaluating a dog or a horse or one of his cotton plants. If only he knew.

"Not bad? Most people would . . ."

"Would what?"

"Oh, nothing." She'd been part of a celebrity charity fund-raiser last year in America, and the guests had paid $500 each to be there.

"No, you were going to say something. Go on. Most people would what?" He watched her with a half smile lighting his face.

Stella's mind raced. "Most people would be offended by a crack like that," she said. " 'Not bad,' indeed! Ha! Go and fix the barbecue."

"May I have my appetizers first, please?" he asked plaintively. "The barbie won't take long."

Stella smiled and sat down. She stuck a celery stick into the dip.

He peered into the little dish. "What's in this?"

"Better you don't know." She bit the end off the celery. Her eyes sparkled at him as she chewed.

"Maybe you're right. I'm concerned how you made it such an interesting color."

"Turmeric," she replied. "You're not overly endowed with spices and stuff. I had to be creative."

"You've done very well." He stuck a whole

square of anchovy toast into his mouth.

Stella watched him cope with the garlic and chili she'd pepped it up with, nearly successfully copying a favorite of Xavier's caterer. She almost choked with laughter on her celery as his eyes widened.

He washed it down with a swill of juice.

"Sorry," she said. "I didn't mean to put so much chili in, but it came out in a *whump,* you know?"

"I do now." He inspected an olive carefully.

"I didn't touch those."

He popped the olive into his mouth. The Eagles finished. Stella got up to change the CD.

"Any preference?" She paused in the doorway.

"No, whatever you'd like."

She'd studied the CD collection earlier. Popular classics, a few jazz albums, some country, and a lot of rock and pop. None of hers, which relieved and disappointed her at the same time.

Now she selected a recording of the Brandenburg Concertos. The crisp, energetic rhythms always cleansed and refreshed her mind.

"I like Bach too," he said as she sat back down at the table. "Those classical CDs were my mother's."

The mother who had run off with a shearer. He didn't appear unwilling to mention her, but Stella chose her words with care. "Doreen told me about your parents, both of them. I'm sorry, it must have been difficult."

"It was very hard for a while," he said briskly.

"How old were you when your mother left?"

He studied her, and she thought he wasn't going to answer, would snap at her instead, but he said, "Fourteen. Keith was sixteen, and Carrie was eleven."

"So your Dad brought you and Keith and your sister up?"

He nodded.

"My Mum brought me up. I'm an only child," she said. "My Dad died too, when I was eleven."

"Is your Mum still alive?"

"She is, but she's in a nursing home. She has dementia."

"She can't be very old."

"She's not. It was early onset. She had me when she was forty-one. She's sixty-seven. She doesn't know who I am anymore, but physically she's very well."

"That's very sad."

"Yes."

"So in a way, you're an orphan too," he said.

"When did your father die?"

"Six years ago. I was in the last year of my degree." He stood up. The chair scraped harshly on the floor as he pushed it away. "I'll get the barbecue going."

Stella collected the remains of the antipasto platter and followed him through to the kitchen, where he was looking in a cupboard under the sink. She dumped the dish onto the counter and leaned against the door frame, enjoying the sight of his rear end as he bent over. He really did have very good muscle tone. Country life had certain benefits. She stifled a giggle, more relaxed now in this masculine company than she had been with anyone for ages. Since . . . she couldn't remember. Not even Mark had sparred with her the way Jonathan did. She had to work hard with Jonathan. He kept her on her toes, made her think, made her interested in him. His natural reserve invited her to probe.

"Matches." He shifted a few objects out of the way. "Aha!"

"Jonathan, how come you're not married?"

"How come you're not?" He straightened,

box of matches in hand. "Sorry — I forgot, you were. Anyway, I nearly was."

"To the designer lady?"

"Lena, yes." His expression indicated that this wasn't a topic he wanted to discuss.

Stella charged on. "But how come you haven't been snapped up by a girl from around here? There must be lots of women who'd leap at you — successful business-man, owns his own company, land, car — of sorts, lovely house, dog, healthy, fit, enterprising, kind, house-trained." She grinned. "Good-looking." He raised an eyebrow, but a small twitch of the lips told her he was flattered. "Doreen says you're the most eligible bachelor for miles, and from what I've seen, it could be true."

She edged out of his way as he moved to the door and smiled up at him, teasing. He stepped closer and stared into her eyes. "There's a shortage of females in the out-back, didn't you know?"

"Is that why you were so keen on my stay-ing here?" Stella's smile widened.

"Did I give you that impression?"

"You did seem very keen."

"And you looked at me as though I was trying to abduct you and seduce you." His tone was teasing too, but, looking into his eyes, Stella read something else, which

126

made her smile fade. Hurt? Disappointment?

"I'm sorry. I was a bit suspicious, but a girl has to be careful."

"Of course. It's sensible, and I understand." He nodded but didn't move away.

"Plus, even when Doreen and Leo said how well respected you were, I didn't know you at all, and a lot of guys . . ." She stopped.

"What? Come on to you?" His voice was husky and gentle now.

Stella nodded. "It's hard to tell whether they mean it or not," she whispered, naked and exposed, under the spotlight, the hurt of the divorce still raw. She glanced up at him, then down quickly as she met his penetrating gaze. "Most don't. One in particular didn't."

Most wanted to be seen on the arm of Stella Starr and to circulate in the world of Stella Starr, whatever they imagined it was. Most didn't give a cracker about her, the girl behind the image. And the one she thought had, hadn't. Very publicly.

"I would've thought a girl as pretty as you would've learned very early on how to deal with a guy she doesn't want," he said, without moving. "And now you can break his arm, if necessary."

Stella stared at him, standing so close in the doorway that she could feel the warmth of his body and smell the light, fresh tang of soap and aftershave. His chest rose and fell as he breathed, and the fine lines around his eyes from the harshness of the elements added character to his face. Those eyes were honest eyes. The thought flashed through her head in an instant. If Jonathan said he loved, he would mean it.

Her gaze traveled from his eyes across the tanned planes of his freshly shaved cheeks to his mouth. His lips were curved in a little smile. How would they feel against hers? Her own breath came tight and fast. He didn't know who she was; she could kiss him to satisfy her own curiosity. She could please herself. Any other girl would. Julianne definitely would, faced with an attractive man who obviously thought she was attractive. And, let's face it, men did find her, as Susanna or Stella, attractive. He'd been trying to hit on her since he first saw her.

She rose on tiptoe, placed her hands on his shoulders, and pressed her lips against his. For a moment she thought he would push her away because he made no response at all. She had just enough time for the words *big mistake* to form in her head. The muscles in his shoulders tensed under her fingers.

Then Stella got the shock of her life as he took control — an electric shock coursing through her frame starting at the point of contact, his lips, and radiating out in crackling, hissing sparks. Her mind short-circuited, and a small groan escaped from deep in her body as Jonathan gripped her firmly. She lost track of time, lost track of place, lost track of herself and what she'd meant to achieve by starting this explosive chain reaction.

Then he stopped abruptly, let her go. His breath came in short, ragged bursts as he gazed at her, green eyes gone dark, brows angled down in a frown.

"Why did you do that?" he asked hoarsely. To Stella's amazement he sounded angry.

"I wanted to," she gasped before she could think of anything else. He'd done most of it. What was he talking about?

"Maybe I'm an old-fashioned country boy, but I prefer to take the initiative." He shook his head as if to rid himself of her touch.

"Didn't take you long to catch up," Stella snapped. "Sorry, I didn't mean to frighten you."

"I don't scare very easily." He pushed past

her. "I'd better light the barbecue."

Stella stayed in the kitchen, tears of rage filming her eyes. Of all the stupid, stiff-necked, old-fashioned country yokels — why couldn't he just admit he'd enjoyed kissing her? Why did he have to play macho man? It was only a kiss! A mind-boggling, toe-curling, nuclear meltdown of a kiss but still . . .

She clenched her hands into fists and stomped out to the back courtyard where he was standing next to the barbecue watching a tiny flicker of flame begin to swell and glow red in the twilight. The sun had almost set, leaving purple and orange streaks across the western sky in a glorious kaleidoscope. She barely noticed.

"What are you so upset about, for heaven's sake?" she yelled as she came down the veranda steps to the paved area. "What's so bad about a girl's kissing a man first? Crawl into the twentieth century, Jonathan."

Lancelot hauled himself out from under the veranda and watched the entertainment with his tail swishing from side to side.

"It's the twenty-first," Jonathan pointed out in a mild voice.

"You haven't made it to the twentieth yet."

"I don't mind a girl's kissing me first if she's a girl I'm involved with. What, exactly,

130

did you have in mind, Susanna? You could confuse a stupid person, you know, and I'm not stupid, whatever you may think, but you've confused me. First you go on about guys making unwanted advances, and then you kiss me. What am I supposed to think?"

Stella gaped at him, too astonished and bewildered at the direction this conversation had taken, to stay angry. "It was only a friendly kiss," she cried. "A thank you!" It had started out as one on her side.

"Yeah, well." Jonathan poked at the glowing coals. "You took me by surprise. I wasn't sure what you wanted."

"Didn't you like it?" Her voice shrank to a whisper. Surely he did. "I did."

She didn't know what she'd wanted, except now, having gotten it, she wanted more of the same, wanted him to kiss her again. First. But he'd as good as told her she'd made an unwanted advance.

Jonathan stared at her through the gathering darkness. "Of course I liked it," he said eventually. "What man wouldn't?"

"Can we still be friends, then, if I promise not to kiss you?" Stella smiled, but behind the smile was a plea. What did she really know about men? She'd missed out on that formative part of her life. The teenage years of making mistakes, heartbreak and learning, discussions with girlfriends, tips and hints. When to take the initiative, when not. Mark had wooed her and romanced and flattered her into marriage, and she hadn't known what was happening. He seemed to love her so much, she didn't like to disappoint him.

Jonathan gave a little snort, which may have been amusement, but his smile was slightly twisted as well. "Go and get the steaks," he said.

Stella turned and rushed up the steps. The screen door slammed behind her.

He heaved a deep, shuddering sigh and closed his eyes. She'd kissed him. Stella Starr had kissed him of her own free will, and he'd totally blown it by turning a friendly thank-you kiss into a passionate smooch. How close had he come to going further? Very.

Talk about playing with fire. She was in a league all her own, and he was a child by comparison. She and her world-weary crowd would throw kisses and hugs around like popcorn, signifying nothing. To her it would mean zip, nada, zilch, zero.

In which case, he needn't worry. He could file the memory away for future reference and tell his mates he'd kissed Stella Starr. And she was one hot kisser. This memory would keep him awake tonight, especially with her across the passage in Carrie's room.

Of course the bottom line to this whole situation was, he needed to keep her happy and relaxed so she would be amenable to the Koolwear thing when he suggested it. He couldn't possibly start anything with her in her guise of Susanna, because then everything would become horribly complicated. More horribly complicated. He mustn't touch her or let her touch him.

The last thing he wanted was for her to *really* think he'd brought her out to Jingaluck to seduce her, Susanna or Stella. He wanted nothing for her to use against him when the time came. It was going to be difficult enough without sex getting in the way.

The outside light came on, and the door opened. Jonathan glanced up as she walked carefully down the wooden steps holding a covered plate. He hoped she hadn't done anything exotic to the steaks — marinated them in ginger wine and oyster sauce or some such. Then he saw the expression on her face, and his newly formed resolution wilted.

She looked like a little girl, tentative, eager to please, totally unsure of herself. He remembered the tone of her voice when she asked him if he liked kissing her. What sort of question was that? From Stella Starr? But then, she was playing at being Susanna, and Susanna could well be a naïve girl. In her mind, she could be trying to reclaim her lost innocence, or some such new-age rubbish. She spent a lot of her time in LA, after all.

Don't touch her. He had to keep the thought uppermost in his mind.

"I marinated the steak." Her voice held a hint of uncertainty.

"I hate to think in what." He smiled at her to show he was being friends.

"In red wine, garlic, herbs, and olive oil. It's a very good marinade, I'll have you know." Her bottom lip firmed with indignation.

"It's a very good steak," he said. "So it had better be. I'll get the tongs."

"I forgot to bring out the onions. They're on the counter in the blue bowl."

He turned toward the house, tousling Lancelot's ears as he went by. The old dog's tail waved gently to and fro.

Stella wandered across to the pool at the edge of the light from the veranda. She stared up into the darkening sky, searching for stars. The night air still held the heat of the day, and warmth radiated up from the paving stones under her feet. So peaceful out here. It was wonderful.

The screen door banged. He came down the steps holding the blue bowl and long silver tongs. He threw the two steaks, dripping marinade, onto the grill. A cloud of steam rose up, and he flapped a hand before his face.

"Smells good," he called.

"Nothing beats a barbecue on a hot summer night," she said. "It hasn't cooled down at all, has it?"

"We can have a swim later."

She wandered to where he stood overseeing their cooking dinner. "Pity we can't eat outside. At least the air's fresher."

"We can now it's dark."

"What about mosquitoes?"

"I was joking. Did you notice any last night?"

"No. Good. I'll bring everything out." She went to the kitchen and found a tray on which to load their plates, cutlery, the salads and sauces, then maneuvered her way back outside and down the steps.

"Watch out." Jonathan darted forward, tongs in hand.

Stella's bare legs collided with soft, furry Lancelot, who decided at that precise moment to stroll across her path and stop. The plates slid on the heavy tray. She desperately tried to right it before she lost the lot.

Jonathan, reaching to assist, dropped the tongs on Lancelot's head. The dog gave a surprised yelp and scuttled out of the way, leaving Jonathan and Stella clutching the tray, hopping about in a kind of mad dance. He took the tray to the safety of the table.

Stella drew a shaky breath. "I nearly dropped our whole dinner. Silly dog, I nearly squashed you!" she called to Lancelot, who had sat down to watch from a safe distance.

She retrieved the tongs and inspected them. "These will need a wash."

"Hurry up, because the rest of our dinner will burn soon if I don't turn it over."

"Yes, boss." Stella raced inside to the kitchen. When she came back out, he took the tongs and handed her a glass in exchange.

"Here's to a successful dinner," he said.

"Hear, hear."

Sparkling eyes met his as they clinked glasses. Jonathan gazed at her. She was an extraordinary woman, so forgiving, so gentle and undemanding, but with her own integrity and strength. She'd returned his flaring passion with what felt like equal passion of her own. Real passion. Her body had molded itself to his; she'd tasted so sweet, smelled so wonderful. There couldn't be a next time. How he would give everything for a next time.

"The onions are burning, chef," she said.

CHAPTER SIX

Jonathan darted to rescue the onions, which had begun sending up little smoke signals of distress. He flipped the steaks while he was at it, attempting to look busy and competent and unconcerned, trying to hide his racing pulse and clammy hands. *Stupid!*

"It's lovely out here at night." She had moved to sit on the tiled edge of the pool, trailing a hand in the water. "I had another swim earlier. I couldn't resist, it's been so unbearably hot."

"I usually go in at night. Lie on my back and stargaze."

"Aah. Fabulous."

"More fun with someone else. And I don't mean Keith and Renata."

He caught the glimmer of her teeth in the light from the veranda as she smiled. "I can imagine."

He cleared his throat. "These steaks are ready. I'm assuming you don't like yours well done, and even if you did, I wouldn't let you have it that way."

"Lucky for me, I don't."

Stella sprang up and hurried to the table. She whipped the covers off the salads and sat down as Jonathan forked a juicy, steaming chunk of meat onto her plate.

"Good grief, there's half a bullock here."

"What you can't eat, Lancelot will," he replied.

Lancelot had taken up a position by the table where he could keep both diners under observation.

"He's got his begging spot picked already. It must be terribly tantalizing for the poor old boy," she said.

Lancelot gazed at her dolefully and licked his lips.

"He's too fat. Lazy devil."

"He's old and retired; he deserves a rest."

"From what?" Jonathan laughed. "You're too softhearted, Susanna."

"Must be my city girl attitude." She spooned potato salad onto her plate. "I love potatoes, and I'm hardly ever allowed to have them, especially with mayonnaise."

"Why aren't you allowed to have spuds? They're a staple. You need spuds for energy. Anyway, who says you can't?"

Stella cut off a chunk of steak. That was

the trouble with relaxing; she forgot to censor her tongue. She shoved the food in and chewed slowly. Maybe Jonathan would start talking about something else. He didn't. He waited, serving himself salad in the interim. Then he looked at her, eyebrows raised expectantly.

"Spuds? Why not?" he prompted.

"I've just lost heaps of weight. I have to be careful. I used to be enormous. Massive."

"Must have lost a lot. Do you think you may have overdone it a bit?"

"You accused me of being heavy!" she cried. "As if you could barely lift me."

He grinned. "And you fell for it."

"If I don't watch what I eat, I'll explode outward again, and you'll never be able to get me off the ground."

"I could give it a try. I'm pretty strong."

He looked her in the eye, and her stomach tightened. A tingle of something fluttered down her spine. Something wonderful.

"I know," she said softly.

Jonathan held her gaze. She held her breath. He picked up his knife and fork and sliced into the steak.

She exhaled in a shaky release of tense muscles and tortured lungs. What was he doing to her? What was happening here? This was a man she hardly knew, a man she'd kissed on impulse and who'd kissed her like a full-blown Casanova, then told her off for being wanton. Now he seemed to be flirting with her. Was this his way of getting around to making the first move in his country boy way?

All right. She could make it easy for him. As long as it didn't get out of hand. But if he kissed her again, there was no telling what might happen. If he kissed her at all, that was, because she certainly wasn't making the same humiliating mistake again.

"So," she said, "are we skinny-dipping after dinner?"

"I've got a swimming costume," he replied after a moment of surprised silence.

Stella squashed the last of the potato salad onto her fork, savoring the taste as it slid over her tongue. She pulled the fork out, watching Jonathan. His expression was priceless. Alarm mixed with embarrassment mixed with surprise.

She couldn't stifle the laugh. "You suggested it."

He made a good recovery. "I know you better now."

She frowned as if considering the point. "That should make it more all right, not less."

"If you want to swim nude, go ahead.

Finished?" He picked up her empty plate and began loading the tray.

She leaned back in her chair and smiled, but he gave her a stern look and went into the house.

"He's embarrassed, Lancelot. I've embarrassed your lord and master." Stella rubbed the old dog's ears. She walked to the pool, then glanced at the house. No sign of Jonathan. She giggled, quickly stripped off her shirt and shorts to reveal Caroline's swimming costume. The evening air danced warm and soft on her bare skin.

She raised her arms overhead, stretched up full length on her toes, then dived in a flat arc into the dark water. Deeper down it was cool against her legs. Wonderful. She came to the surface gasping and blowing bubbles. She trod water for a moment and watched the house. Jonathan appeared, moving against the lighted window, then disappeared. The back door slammed, and his steps sounded on the paving.

She lay back and floated, staring up into the inky darkness studded with thousands upon thousands of glittering diamonds. The moon was just rising through the trees on the far slope. Glorious, glorious night.

The back door slammed again. She swiveled about to stare toward the house. He'd gone inside. Pity. She resumed floating, eyes closed, arms spread wide. She drifted, aimless, totally relaxed, free. Then she heard him come out and walk toward her. She kept her eyes closed and allowed herself to soar — such a wonderful feeling, no constraints, no pressure, gently supported in the warmth of the water.

"Come in, the water's wonderful," she called, eyes still shut, senses wide open.

"I'd better not." His voice was harsh, shattering the stillness. "I brought you a towel."

"Why had you better not?" Stella jackknifed and swam across to where he stood staring down at her, his body a darker shape against the brighter outline of the house. His face was a black mask, although he'd be able to see her pale body in the water.

"I just don't think it's a good idea." He didn't move.

"I promise not to kiss you." She lay on her back and pulled away with slow, lazy strokes, knowing he was watching.

"That's not what . . ." he called, but Stella didn't hear the rest because she touched the end of the pool and duck dived to return underwater. When she surfaced, he'd gone.

She floated a while longer, then dragged herself out and lay on the edge. The tiles still retained heat from the day, warm under her back and legs. She closed her eyes. Perhaps she could sleep outdoors tonight. On the veranda.

Lancelot sniffed at her wet hair, puffing doggy breath on her face. She giggled and sat up. He plopped onto his haunches, grinning and panting. She picked up the towel, wrapped it around her waist, and trailed back to the house with her clothes draped over her arm. Why hadn't Jonathan swum with her? More fun with someone else, he'd said. Why not with her?

Jonathan was in the kitchen making coffee. He glanced up when she stopped in the doorway. He'd done the dishes. He smiled, but his expression was cool. Then his eyes ran swiftly up and down her body, registering the bathing suit.

He grinned. "You . . ." He laughed, shaking his head. The wonderful something pierced her heart again. "Enjoy your swim?"

"Yes." Heart so full, words wouldn't form.

"I was always told never to go swimming after a meal."

"For an hour," agreed Stella. "But no one ever said why. What do you think will happen to me?"

"If anything was going to happen, it would've already. Cramps. While you were in the water," he said. "Coffee will be served

144

in the living room."

"I'll go change."

Stella went to the bathroom to dispose of the wet towel and swimsuit. She took a very short shower and applied body lotion and moisturizer. Bore water was hard on the skin. She dragged her brush through her hair, which was half dry already, but left it down around her shoulders. She grimaced. Pale brown roots were beginning to show.

"How do you like your coffee?" asked Jonathan.

"Black, thanks."

He poured and handed her a cup with a saucer. It had a pattern of pink roses around the rim. She settled herself on the couch, leaving plenty of room for him to join her.

"I'm really enjoying my stay. I don't know how I'll ever repay you all for your kindness."

He sat in the chair facing her. "I'll think of something."

"I'm a total stranger. I could be an escaped criminal or a lunatic, for all you know, and here you are, inviting me into your home."

"Give me some credit for character assessment!" Jonathan smiled.

"The same could be said for you, of

course," she said. "Although if we're both lunatics or criminals, then there's no problem."

"We'd be made for each other."

Jonathan's expression changed as he spoke. He stared right into her eyes. Stella met his gaze, still joking. "A match made in heaven."

"Why are you out here at the hottest time of the year? Honestly," he asked softly.

The laughter died in her throat. His gaze never wavered, eyes narrowed, lounging in his chair, legs crossed, coffee cup suspended.

Stella swallowed. She placed her cup, in its pretty saucer, on the magazine-strewn table between them.

"I've just been divorced, and I needed to get away. By myself."

He nodded slowly, considering her reply. Encouraged by his silence, she said, "I shouldn't have married him in the first place, but I was young and naïve, and I thought he loved me. Loved *me,* not . . ."

"Not what?"

She hesitated. "The idea of love, maybe?" She shrugged. "He was so keen to get married, I didn't like to disappoint him." She glanced at Jonathan.

He gave a sharp snort of derision and sat

up straighter. "How ridiculous! No wonder it failed. You mean you married someone because he wanted to marry you, and you didn't want to say no in case he was upset?"

She nodded. Her lower lip trembled. "Silly." The understatement of the year?

He nodded back, total disbelief on his face.

"But I wanted to be looked after. And I have trouble saying no sometimes. *Had* trouble saying no," she corrected. "I thought I was in love. I won't make the same mistake again, that's for sure!" She just substituted other mistakes instead.

"I should hope not." Jonathan paused. "It's why I'm still single, despite, as you so accurately pointed out, my being the most desirable bachelor for many hundreds of kilometers in any direction you care to point. I want to be absolutely sure."

But he filed away her odd remark. She wanted to be looked after? Surely she'd have all sorts of minders and agents looking after her. But that's not what she meant, was it? She was lonely. Lost and lonely. No parents to guide her. An only child. No family at all.

She said, "I've decided to be more assertive and only do things *I* want to do, not what other people expect me to."

"Good for you. I always do."

"So I see. You're a very strong person. You must be to have achieved what you have."

Jonathan's heart sank like a lump of uncooked dough. He was romanticizing and fantasizing. What did he really know about her? She wouldn't want to be Miss Koolwear. She sat there looking gorgeous and self-contained with her damp hair wispy around her neck and funny little untamed curls springing about her forehead, bare legs curled under her on the couch, sipping coffee, smiling a private little smile — crushing his hopes.

If only she wasn't so irresistible. If only she hadn't kissed him. Far better never to have known what he was missing out on.

"What are you thinking?" she asked suddenly.

"I'm wishing you hadn't kissed me," he said with total candor.

She nearly spilled her remaining coffee. She put the cup down. Hurt, and the painfully vulnerable little-girl look, passed over her face before she quickly adopted a cynical expression. "Thanks very much."

He sat forward, his voice tight and urgent in his throat. "Because now I want to kiss you again, and I know it wouldn't be the right thing to do."

"Wouldn't it?"

"Definitely not."

Stella uncurled her legs slowly from under her. Her slim fingers went to her Koolwear blouse and adjusted the neckline as she straightened up. The silence intensified; somehow the room temperature had risen. A trickle of perspiration ran down his side.

She slid forward and stood up, then came around the table to where he sat mesmerized by the sheer grace and beauty of her body, the way she moved. She seemed to glide. She squatted beside him, and he smelled the perfume of her glowing skin. She smiled and leaned on the arm of his chair, closer until their faces were inches apart.

"What if I kiss you again?" she whispered. "Would that be the wrong thing too?"

Jonathan held his breath. The brocade fabric of the old armchair was rough under his hypersensitive fingertips. He exhaled, then looked beyond her at the cluster of photos on the piano. Keith and Renata getting married. His father. If she came any closer, he'd be completely undone. If she kissed him. He swallowed, keeping his eyes away from her sweet face, blocked the intoxicating scent of her body from his nose. When he spoke, his voice was strained.

"Susanna, I would love nothing more than to kiss you again. I'm very flattered that you want to kiss me. But I don't want to take advantage of you. You're recently divorced, you're alone and vulnerable at the moment, emotionally vulnerable. I don't want to complicate your life. It would be a meaningless and pointless exchange. You're here for the weekend at most, and I . . ."

He leaped from the chair as though it were an ejector seat or a rocket launcher and, before he knew it, was on the far side of the couch. Stella had fallen back onto her bottom on the floor during his rush to extricate himself, and she sat there now, staring at him in bewilderment, as well she might.

Meaningless and pointless exchange? Where had that come from? Kissing her would never be meaningless, and there would most definitely be a point to it. A point he would reach with exquisite and immeasurable delight.

"Well, there's a first," she said in a strangled voice. "I guess you've made your position very clear. I'm sorry to have forced myself upon you again, although I can't see what your problem is, apart from an overdeveloped sense of decency, I thought a kiss or two might be rather nice, and we are consenting adults."

150

Her face was pink, the telltale quaver of tears in her voice despite the bravado of the words. She leaned back on her extended arms, sniffed once, loudly, and jumped to her feet with a hasty wipe across her eyes with the back of one hand.

He said, "I'm sorry. I guess I'm just not that type of guy. We're a bit slower to move out here in the backblocks. We don't play fast and loose."

"I see. Now."

"But don't think it's because you're not attractive — you are, very. It's because I don't —"

Stella held up a hand. "Stop. It's fine. I understand. You're a gentleman. I'm a loose-living city girl looking for a bit of fun."

She dropped onto the couch with her back to him and picked up an old copy of *Farmer's Weekly*. She stared at it as though desperate to learn all about sheep dips and crop dusting.

Jonathan gritted his teeth and drew a deep breath. *Wrong, wrong, wrong. She understood nothing!* If it wasn't for the factory and all the people relying on him, he'd have her in his bed so fast, she wouldn't know what had happened until she came up for air on Monday. *Gentleman?* No one had ever accused him of being a gentleman before, and he'd never been taken for a bumbling, fumbling country boy either.

"Time for me to hit the sack. We farmers get up early."

"Mind if I stay up?" She gave him a bright, superficial smile, the magazine open on her lap.

"Not at all. Make yourself at home." How was he going to sleep?

"Do you have to work tomorrow? It's Saturday."

"The factory closes, but farms never stop. I have to check some pipes in one of the far fields. Be out most of the day. Will you be all right here by yourself?"

"Of course. I'll do what I did this afternoon — swim and read, just like at a holiday resort."

"Well . . . good night. Enjoy yourself. We'll go to the pub tomorrow night for karaoke."

"I'd rather go to the outdoor movies," said Stella. "It sounded like fun."

"Oh."

"But whatever you like," she said swiftly.

No way would he spend another evening alone with her, not side by side in the dark at the movies. He didn't have deck chairs; he and his dates took a blanket and cushions — and hardly watched the movie. Anyway, she had to get to know the townspeople, see how reliant they were on the success of Koolwear. They had to become real to her. People. Friends. The pub was the social center of the area.

And then he could tell her quietly that they all knew who she was. With any luck she'd trust everyone enough to keep her secret and not be too upset.

"Forecast said rain's on the way, so we may not have a choice. Good night." He smiled and headed for his bedroom, where he closed the door and flung himself onto his bed, sprawled diagonally, feet dangling over the edge. *Of all the prize idiots!* Why couldn't he have just given her a chaste little kiss instead of insulting her and making her feel cheap, unwanted, and, worst of all, undesirable?

He'd put her in an impossible position. She was a guest in his house. He'd kissed her with an accumulated twelve years' worth of dormant passion. Unleashed all the stored-up longing and desire, when she would've expected a platonic brush of the lips, a thank-you kiss. And then he'd compounded it by telling her he wished he'd never kissed her. By extension she could assume that he meant he wished she'd never kissed him. Which was true — but not for any of the reasons so far stated.

He thumped his fists on the bed, sat up slowly, and removed his shoes and socks. He pulled his shirt off and dropped it to the floor, then slid off the bed and went to the bathroom to wash his face and brush his teeth. Music came softly from the living room. She was playing a jazz CD now — Jim Hall Trio — one of his favorites.

He switched off the light and stepped into the hallway. Stella was standing right outside the door. Jonathan stopped abruptly. "Oh. Gosh. You startled me."

Her gaze flew to his bare chest, then away to a point on the wall beside him. "Sorry." She flushed pink. "I was just waiting for . . ." She indicated the bathroom but didn't move to go in.

Jonathan waited. Stella stood there, small, unsure. He bent down without thinking and kissed her warm cheek. She didn't move. He raised his hand to her mouth and brushed her soft lips with his fingertips.

"You are the most beautiful woman I've ever seen," he whispered. "You could have any man you wanted."

Stella lifted her gaze to his. Her mouth trembled under his touch as she smiled. "I don't think so. But you're not too bad yourself," she whispered back.

Her eyes grew soft and moist. He dropped

his hand to his side before his fingers could slip around her neck and draw her close, draw her into his embrace and into his kiss.

"Good night," he murmured.

"Good night." She went into the bathroom.

Jonathan lay on his bed with a sheet over his legs. The air in the bedroom was stifling and oppressive. He got up to push the window wider. His pillow was uncomfortable, the bed hot and sticky. He turned over. And over again. Stella's face swam before his eyes. Her lovely smile and the little crinkle at the corner of her mouth. Those gorgeous dark brown eyes.

She seemed keen to have a weekend dalliance in the country. It'd be a novel experience for her. Or maybe it wouldn't. She enjoyed teasing him — the skinny-dipping, for example, when all along she wore a swimming costume and had no intention of stripping off in front of him. Cheeky thing. He smiled ruefully. He'd walked right into it, much to her delight. Stella was an extraordinary and complicated woman. That was one of the things he loved about her.

Jonathan sighed and sat up. He pummeled his unusually lumpy pillow. He lay down again. A door opened and closed. The toilet flushed. The door opened and closed again.

He peered at the green luminous numbers on the bedside clock. 12:03 A.M.

She'd be used to staying up late. Musicians and entertainers always did. They were night workers. Not like farmers. He'd be exhausted tomorrow if he didn't get some sleep.

He mustn't mess up this situation. There was far too much at stake, not least of it Stella's emotional balance. He'd spoken the truth when he told her he wouldn't take advantage of her, so soon after her divorce, unsure of her feelings, adrift and vulnerable. Just because he was bursting with lust and had been since he'd laid eyes on her in the pub.

He still couldn't believe it. Not really. Stella Starr in his house, preparing his dinner, trying to please him with her dubious domestic skills, kissing him, suggesting jokingly they swim naked in his pool. Wanting to kiss him again. Refusing her?!

He woke at five, the clock radio blaring, intruding into his dreams — a bizarre mix of a smiling Stella extolling the virtues of fresh-lemon–fragranced washing detergent, Koolwear, and himself swimming in a pool with all his clothes on, being dragged under the water.

The sheet was twisted around his legs, and

his pillow was on the floor. He disentangled himself and grabbed his robe to visit the bathroom. Then, clad in old gray swimming shorts and carrying a towel, he padded outside into the fresh morning air and plunged into the welcoming chill of the pool. The sun hadn't risen above the eastern rise of hills yet, but shafts of pink and pale yellow indicated dawn was imminent. A mass of clouds had built up overnight. Rain later with any luck. It had been hot enough. They were due for a storm. Magpies chortled in the stand of pines, and a flock of pink and gray galahs streaked toward the river, dipping and swooping with the sheer joy of life.

He swam up and down for twenty solid minutes, then hauled himself out and sat on the edge to catch his breath. Lancelot wandered over to join him, sitting patiently waiting for his breakfast.

"Hungry?" Lancelot licked his lips and thumped his tail on the ground. "Come on."

Jonathan rubbed his hair and chest with the towel as he strolled back to the house, scanning the pale morning sky. Definite thickening of clouds on the horizon. He hadn't bothered listening to the forecasts for the last few days. Since Stella's arrival, the world outside Koologong and Jingaluck had almost ceased to exist.

The sun had edged over the horizon and already held a promise of the forthcoming heat. If only he could stay home with her — but that would entail not only tempting fate but also neglecting his work. He did need to go out to the far fields and check the watering system. Grant, from the neighboring property, was meeting him. One of the pumps wasn't working properly. They'd have to pull it apart, fiddle around finding the problem, then attempt to fix it. Keith normally took care of those sorts of things.

The kitchen radio was on. He heard the clink of cutlery. Stella? His heart pounded as he draped the towel casually around his neck, gripping the ends with tense fingers.

She smiled at him. Bright, cheerful, fresh as the morning dew, wearing her shorts and a pink tank top, hair in the ponytail again, all traces of last night's drama gone and forgotten.

"Good morning," he said. "You're up early. Sorry, did I wake you?"

"No, no. I woke up early and did some training while you were swimming. Too hot later, and I really feel it when I don't do any exercise. I'm used to it, and early morning's the best part of the day in summer, isn't it? It's a gorgeous morning, so fresh after last night. I saw some kangaroos in the paddock."

She stopped as if realizing her words had been flooding out fast and furious. She was nervous too. As nervous as he was, judging by the way her gaze darted about, avoiding his bare chest and legs. More so. He removed the towel from around his neck and tossed it behind him into the laundry. He stretched his arms over his head, then rubbed his chest with both hands and slapped himself on the stomach before sauntering to where she stood.

"What's for breakfast?"

She turned her back, grabbed some bread from the packet, and stuck a couple of slices into the toaster. She rammed the lever down.

"Turn it on at the wall," suggested Jonathan.

She flicked the switch. "Toast, eggs, tea, or coffee," she said, still with her back turned. "How do you like your eggs? Fried, scrambled, boiled, or poached?"

"Scrambled with bacon, please. And tea."

"Right."

Stella fought to keep her voice level as she reeled off the breakfast menu. If he moved away, she could get to the cupboard with the frying pans and saucepans without turning and facing his tanned chest, muscular shoulders and arms, and flat belly above the waistband of his tatty old swimmers. His hair was tousled from the swim and the rub of the towel. He hadn't shaved yet that morning, and the fine stubble shadowing his jaw and cheeks enhanced the strength of his features and the softness of his full-lipped mouth. She knew what those lips felt like; she knew what passion lurked beneath the laid-back exterior.

But he wasn't the man for her. Rather, more accurately, she wasn't the woman for him. Jonathan Knight was a gentleman. He'd turned her down in the nicest way by saying he didn't want to take advantage of her. Lots of men would have in his position. She'd thrown herself at him like the cheapest and most desperate of women, and he'd fended her off with the utmost tact, telling her she was beautiful and, despite being very tempted, he had declined — for her sake. He'd proven to her by that very action that he was a man in a million. One with integrity and values, a man to be loved, a man whose love was to be treasured. A sexy man. A perfect man.

Stella had decided during her hot and restless night that she had to prove to Jonathan she was not the helpless, impractical, messed-up, amoral city girl she had thus far displayed to him, but a practical, competent, and useful woman. One he would be proud to know. Starting with breakfast.

She turned with a brisk, "You go and get dressed, and I'll have breakfast ready when you are." She nipped past him and opened the fridge before she got another eyeful of his body, studying the contents until she heard his bare feet pad out the door and down the corridor toward his room. He returned almost immediately, surprising her so much, the eggs she was holding almost slipped from her grasp to smash on the floor.

"Forgot to feed Lancelot." He stood next to her at the open fridge — so close that his bare arm brushed hers. The tang of bore water on his skin coupled with the heady scent of maleness filled her nostrils and addled her brain. He leaned down and grabbed a plastic container.

"Don't cook this up by mistake." He closed the fridge door, collected a spoon from the drawer, and went outside, calling Lancelot.

Stella deposited the eggs safely on the counter and exhaled, leaning back against the sink for support. This man — this man, Jonathan — she'd thought about him most of the night, had listened with straining ears for any sign he might come to her room, knowing he wouldn't, praying he would, and ultimately pleased he hadn't because it proved he meant what he said about not taking advantage of her situation.

Now, in the cold light of morning, seeing him in the flesh and most of it tantalizingly exposed, all she could think of was his kiss. Her bare arm had brushed his, and he laughed into her eyes. And now, standing in the kitchen, shaking and breathless, with a crash of internal thunder and a lightning strike to her heart, she realized what had happened. As the French so aptly put it, she'd had *a coup de foudre.* Love at first sight, or at least first kiss.

Brain not connecting with mouth, either babbling incoherently or freezing entirely. Clammy hands. The shakes when he was near. An intense desire to touch the body of the man in question, wanting to please him, wanting him to like her so much that it hurt. She'd sung about it often enough. Was this love?

If it was, she'd never been in love before. And if it was, she'd fallen in love with Jonathan Knight sometime between dinner last night and now.

But she couldn't tell him. She could never

let on how she felt because to him she was Susanna Starkey, slightly confused, emotionally damaged city girl, and if he found out who she really was, he'd be furious at being duped and would think even less of her than he did now. He'd think she was playing around with him for some twisted reason of her own.

Maybe she was.

No, far better to maintain the Susanna image of a woman not averse to a kiss or two but willing to be friends regardless. The most she could expect from Jonathan was that he think her a good sort and that he liked her. It was very important, his good opinion.

CHAPTER SEVEN

When Jonathan returned to the kitchen in his work clothes — khaki shorts and a well-worn black and white checked shirt with the sleeves rolled up and a top button missing — Stella had toast and tea ready on the table, bacon sizzling, and scrambled eggs warming in the pan.

She served him with a flourish.

"Looks pretty good." He shook pepper all over the eggs.

Stella poured two cups of tea. She sat opposite him and spread marmalade on a slice of toast.

"What are you doing today?"

"Have to check one of the pumps. Watering's crucial, so we can't afford to have a pump break down for long."

"May I come?" Jonathan looked up in surprise. Stella met his gaze firmly. "I'd really like to. If I wouldn't be in the way."

"You'll get bored."

"No, I won't. I might be able to help."

"Have you got any proper shoes? And a shirt would be better than that top. I can lend you a hat."

"I've got trainers. Why?"

"Those sandals won't last five minutes out here, and they're not much protection against snakes."

She jumped up. "I'll change."

"Finish your breakfast first. And eat more than one piece of toast." He accompanied the directive with a stern frown.

Stella obediently took another piece of toast. "Do we need to take lunch with us?"

"No, we'll come back here. Might not need to go out this afternoon if we get the thing fixed. Too hot anyway. I've got some accounts and paperwork to do."

Stella sat next to Jonathan in the red ute. They drove past the house in the opposite direction from the driveway, on a dirt road that wound over the hill and alongside acres and acres of cotton plants growing in neat rows. After about fifteen minutes he turned left, and they drove between the fields until a line of trees rose in the distance.

"Is that the river?"

"Yes. We're allowed to pump a certain amount of water out each year. The government has meters on the pumps to check what we use. I think the meter might be the problem."

They pulled up in the shade of a magnificent, massive old gum tree close to a small shed. A pipe extended down toward the river and disappeared. Stella peered down the steep bank at the muddy water flowing sluggishly past. A line of weary gums lined the river. Fallen bark and leaves crackled under her feet. The ubiquitous cicadas roared overhead. Good thing Jonathan had told her to wear solid shoes. A snake could easily be lying here masquerading as a stick, sunning himself. It was ten minutes to eight, and already it was hot.

She adjusted the old Akubra Jonathan had stuck on her head as they walked to the ute. "Suits you," he'd said, as he opened the door for her.

"Is it very deep?" she asked now.

"In places. During the dry, the level dropped a lot, but it's come up a bit lately." He squinted at the sky. White billowy clouds had gathered in a thick band along the horizon. "Might get a bit of rain later."

The sound of an engine made her glance around. A plume of dust heralded the approach of another vehicle through the expanse of green. Jonathan said, "This'll be

Grant. He's the expert on things mechanical."

She raised an eyebrow. "Better than Dan?"

He laughed. "Everybody's better than Dan."

"What!?"

"Just kidding."

Too hasty a response in her opinion. She followed him to the little shed and watched through the door as he poked about with something connected to the engine. An old white station wagon arrived in a cloud of dust. A large man extricated himself from the front seat. A blue heeler jumped out and ran across to the gum trees, sniffing the ground enthusiastically.

"G'day," the man said. "You must be Sue. Grant Oliver."

He stuck out his hand and grasped hers in his large paw. Stella smiled and did the best she could in terms of returning his grip. Her hand had almost disappeared. The dog ran back to sniff at her legs.

"Git back, Blue," Grant snapped. The dog slunk away and flopped down in the shade by the shed.

"How did you know my name?" she asked. Then she smiled. Silly question. Everyone within a hundred-mile radius would know not only her name, but where she was staying and why. Probably knew yesterday, before she did.

Jonathan bellowed from the shed. "Get a move on, you layabout!"

"Yes, sir," barked Grant. He winked at Stella.

"Lazy so and so. We've been here for hours." Jonathan appeared in the doorway.

"We have not," said Stella.

Grant laughed and shook his head. "Don't take any notice of him, Sue. No one else does. What do you reckon's wrong?" This last question was directed at Jonathan.

"I think it's the new meter, choking the flow somehow."

"Well, it's one way of restricting water usage, I suppose."

The two men disappeared into the shed, discussing the problem. Stella turned away and wandered along the bank. The dog heaved himself to his feet and followed.

Grant came out and took something from the back of the station wagon. Clunking and the odd curse emanated from the shed. She sat under a tree and idly threw sticks into the water. The dog squatted nearby with his pink tongue lolling. The cicadas sang overhead, a deafening noise in the otherwise silent expanses.

A melody popped into her head. She

hummed it under her breath. Nice. She'd recorded most of her own tunes. Others floated about in her head and on various pages of manuscript and notebooks back in the oceanfront apartment. She needed pencil and paper to jot down the rhythm and the melody line. Words would come later.

She stood up, dusted her bottom free of twigs, and went to the shed. The men had removed the cover from the pump and were fiddling with a pipe.

"I think the filter might be blocked," Grant said.

"You reckon?"

"Yeah, could be. Nothing's wrong with the pump itself."

"Have to get down there and clean it out." Jonathan glanced up as Stella's shadow fell across the doorway. He smiled, and his expression softened as he looked at her. "Getting bored?"

"No. Anything I can do?"

"Take off your boots and hop into the river," suggested Grant.

"Really? Shall I?"

"No!" cried Jonathan.

"Why can't I?"

"It's slippery and muddy, and apart from anything else, you don't know what to do."

"You wouldn't be strong enough," added Grant. "We've gotta lift the pipe up and get the filter off. Weighs a ton."

"We do it?" asked Jonathan.

"Yeah, better give it a go." Grant picked up a wrench from the floor. Disappointed not to be of any use, Stella moved back so they could leave the shed.

"Is there any paper and a pencil in the ute, Jonathan?"

"Paper? A notebook do? There's one in the glove box." He gave her a curious look but didn't ask why she wanted paper. "Sure you're not bored? I can take you back if you like."

"No. It's lovely out here. Sure I can't help?"

"Positive. But thanks." He smiled into her eyes again.

Stella smiled right back, and her heart swelled.

Jonathan turned and followed Grant to the pipe that angled down the steep bank to the water. They took off their boots and socks and stood together muttering, then slipped and slid from Stella's sight, hanging on to the pipe for support. She opened the ute door and rummaged about in the glove compartment. There was chewing gum, which she raided, a ballpoint pen, some dockets, rubber bands, a pair of heavy-duty work gloves, a few coins, a torch, and a notebook.

Stella flipped through to find blank pages. Jonathan's writing sloped forward in neat, even rows. Without the intention of prying, she discovered he'd jotted down reminders about deliveries, quantities of fertilizer, phone numbers, and all manner of random bits and pieces. Peeking into his life that way, seeing the real working man, warmed her heart. Such a personal thing, this notebook, intimate almost. She stared at it with a slight smile.

She carefully removed half a dozen spare pages. Armed with the pen, she went to sit under her tree and watch the maintenance men, humming her new melody and writing down notes and rhythms to remind herself later, when she could get at Jonathan's old piano.

He and Grant were thigh deep in the river, struggling to unscrew the filter and get it up onto the bank. Some creative language came floating by on the rapidly heating air. As the sun rose higher, she moved several times to remain in the shade. The dog went to sleep stretched out flat beside her.

Stella wrote and watched and hummed and yawned. She took her hat off and leaned her back against the rough bark of the tree, gazing up into the shimmering leaves over-head. She yawned again. Her eyes drooped shut.

"She's asleep," Grant said. "Like a baby."

"Not quite. From what I hear, babies wake up every two hours, cry, and wet the bed."

Two male voices guffawed with laughter. Stella blinked awake. She was lying on her side. Two muddy pairs of legs with boots were right in her field of vision. She pushed herself upright. A couple of dead eucalyptus leaves fell from her hair.

"Nice nap?" Jonathan smiled down at her, hands on hips.

"Mmm. Was I asleep for long?" There was red dust on her shirt. She slapped it off in a cloud and stood up. Some country woman she was, sleeping while they worked. Now Jonathan would be convinced of her useless-ness on the land. And she was filthy. With a couple of ants crawling on her legs. She brushed them away.

"About an hour."

"An hour? I'm sorry."

"Why?" said Grant. "You're on holiday. You can please yourself." He and Jonathan exchanged a look that Stella was totally unable to decipher.

"Did you fix it?" she asked. "The pump?"

"Hope so. These yours?" Jonathan bent down and picked up the scattered pages covered in her dots and lines.

"Yes." She grabbed them from his outstretched hand and folded them over before he could examine them more closely.

He glanced at Grant with a grin. "Grant's invited us for lunch over at The Park. I accepted on your behalf."

"Thanks. Thanks very much. I'd love to," she said. Would Jonathan recognize that she'd been writing music? If he did, would he wonder and ask about it? She hadn't told him she did anything musical except work in a shop. "Very kind of you, Grant."

"Jude insisted," he said. "She's the missus. Can't wait to meet you, Sue."

"She doesn't get a lot of visitors." Jonathan gave Grant a stern look. "I'll just shut the shed door, and we'll follow you."

Grant whistled to his doe as he walked to his car. It shot out from the shade of the trees in a blue-gray blur and leaped into the front seat beside him. Stella climbed into the passenger seat of the ute and waited for Jonathan. He tossed the wrench and some other tools into the tray at the back and slid in beside her.

173

"I'm sorry I fell asleep," she said.

"Didn't sleep well last night?"

"Too hot."

"Yes." He looked at her. His eyes were tired. Mud splashes dotted his shirt, and sweat and dust had combined to form lines on his neck and arms.

The intimacy of his gaze made her lower her voice. "Do you have to work this afternoon?"

"I should."

"Why don't we laze around by the pool? Catch up on some sleep."

His eyes bored into hers. Stella ached to reach out and brush the stray flop of hair from his brow, kiss the tiredness from his face.

"I'm not on holiday." His voice came out harshly.

"Do you ever take holidays?" she asked in a normal, conversational tone. She'd forgotten again — no flirting, no trying to seduce him, just friends. She was to be a sensible woman. Not in love.

"Not often. You heard what Renata said. This is their first break for three years."

"I don't very often either. It's difficult."

"Yes. Almost impossible when you run a farm and a business." He started the engine.

"Is Grant's place far?"

"About twenty minutes. We don't have to go."

"Yes, we do. I want to." He smiled when she added, "I can't imagine why his wife's excited about meeting me. I hope she's not disappointed."

The Park nestled in a grove of trees like an oasis. The heat was fierce now with hardly a breath of wind, oppressive like a furnace. The clouds had built up darker and more threatening but were still in the distance. Stella breathed a deep sigh of relief as she stepped into the cool of the long, low-lying house. Like Jingaluck it was surrounded by wide covered verandas, and, as at Jingaluck, the interior was dim, shadowy, and inviting.

"Hello, Sue. How lovely to meet you." An enthusiastic voice burst from the obscurity. Stella lost her hand to a member of the Oliver family for the second time that day. She blinked as her eyes adjusted from glaring sun to indoor shadows.

"Thank you, and likewise." The speaker was short, blond, freckled, rather square, in her late forties, wearing a floral shift and a pair of pink rubber thongs on her feet.

"I bet you'd like a wash." Jude turned her attention to Jonathan and Grant. "And you two need hosing down out in the yard," she

175

added with a raucous shout of laughter. "Filthy beggars. Playing about in mud, by the looks."

She grabbed Stella by one arm and almost dragged her down the corridor to the bathroom. "I've put a clean towel in there for you. Take a shower if you'd like. Use anything — soap, lotions, moisturizer, comb, et cetera. Don't be shy."

"Thanks." Stella suppressed a surge of giggles at the look on Jonathan's face as she was whisked away by this little dynamo. He was the filthy one who'd been working all morning. She was offered a free run in the bathroom, and he was told to hose down in the backyard. "I think a wash will be enough."

"I'm Judy, by the way."

"Yes, Grant told me. Thanks."

Was Judy going to watch her use the toilet and wash herself? The woman stood in the doorway with a beaming smile on her face. It was the same expression Stella often saw on the faces of her fans — blind adoration. They were either struck dumb, or they babbled. Similar to her with Jonathan, when she didn't keep strict control over herself in his presence. When he looked at her a certain way.

She put the plug in the basin and turned

on the tap. Judy stayed rooted to the spot. Stella smiled at her and picked up the soap. Maybe she should ask her to leave. Surely visitors weren't so unusual out here. Judy was acting as if she hadn't seen another woman for years.

"Jude?" boomed Grant's voice from somewhere else in the house.

Her hostess jerked back to reality. "Sorry, excuse me, I'd better go and see to lunch. Sorry."

Stella closed the door with a gentle click and turned the lock. Friendly people, country people. Very friendly — but some were also very odd.

Lunch was served in the kitchen on a large wooden table — a leg of lamb complete with baked potatoes and pumpkin. The table was set for seven.

Stella surveyed the meal in amazement. "How on earth did you survive the heat of the oven?"

"The boys like their roast," Judy said with a cheerful smile. "They'll be in shortly."

"Can I help?"

"No, wouldn't dream of it. I'm all under control. You sit down. You're a guest."

An outer door slammed, and voices and the tread of feet heralded the arrival of "the boys." Three strapping young men, not boys, crowded in, followed by Grant and Jonathan. Broad shoulders, bronzed arms and faces, work shirts and shorts, shy, curious grins as they looked her way. Word had gotten around, all right, about Jonathan's stranded lady visitor.

"These are our boys," said Judy. "Matt, Bill, and Greg."

"Your sons?" Stella shook their proffered hands one by one.

"Yes. They all work on the property. Billy and Matty are doing courses at the tech, and Greggo's finishing up high school this coming year."

The boys settled themselves around the table and began discussing the crop and the weather and the pump and the water situation and everything else connected with growing and producing cotton. It was, Stella decided, like any other farming venture, a risky business, and this family had staked its future on Jonathan's vision. These three young men had committed themselves to Koolwear, as had Jonathan and the rest of the town as far as she could judge.

After lunch the men trooped outside to look at one of the harvesting machines. Stella insisted on helping Judy clear the table and load the dishwasher.

"Are you sure you've had enough to eat?

You hardly ate a thing. Can I get you something else? A sandwich perhaps?"

Stella laughed. "No, it was fine, delicious. I love roast lamb, and I had plenty to eat. You're just used to serving up massive quantities for your men."

"You're right. They eat an enormous amount. I suppose I expect everyone to eat the same way. I'm sure Jonathan doesn't eat enough. He needs a wife. I keep telling him he needs looking after properly."

"Does he? He seems very competent to me." Stella handed a saucepan to Judy to wash in the sink. "And surely Renata and Keith keep an eye on him."

"Yes, of course, but they have their own lives. He worries about the factory and the whole project. It was all his idea, and he feels responsible. Don't get me wrong — we're all behind him one hundred percent, but everyone changed their land over to cotton from other crops or cattle, and if it doesn't work out . . ." She flapped the scourer about vaguely.

"Is it successful?" It hadn't occurred to Stella that it might not be, that Koolwear might be in financial strife beyond the usual struggles of a business venture. "Jonathan seems so competent and confident. I assumed Koolwear was doing well. You've certainly got a good product," she added because it seemed diplomatic and polite.

"Do you think so?" Judy pounced. "Do you *really* think so?" She stared at Stella eagerly.

"Well, yes. Not that my opinion means anything." Stella frowned, surprised by the vehement enthusiasm, and picked up a cloth to wipe down the table.

"Oh, but it does," said Judy in a fluster. "It does. I mean, you're from the city — you're in touch with the latest fashions. You're young — you know what people are wearing. What's popular — fashionable. You dress so beautifully, and you're so elegant. You could be a model." Her face was bright red by this time.

"I'm too short to be a model. I think the famous ones are nearly six feet tall." Stella finished wiping and hung the cloth over the edge of the sink. "Tell me something, Judy. What's Jonathan's sister like — Caroline? I'm sleeping in her room, but Jonathan clams up when her name comes up. Did they fight?"

"Come and sit in the other room — it's cooler." Judy led the way to the living room They sat in large squashy green armchairs, facing each other. "Caroline was always a wild girl. Always in some sort of scrape. Her poor father was at his wit's end. They used to have some ding-dong battles." She lowered her voice to a confidential whisper. "And his drinking didn't help." The voice rose again. "Keith went working up north for a while, and Jonathan went away to university. Caroline was here by herself. She boarded in Walgett and was supposed to come home weekends from school, but she stopped pretty soon. Didn't hardly make it back at all. Then, when she was old enough — just turned seventeen — she hitched a ride and left. I haven't seen her since, and I don't think the Knights have either. I know her father didn't, because he died in that terrible accident soon after. She didn't even come home for the funeral. I don't know why. Jonathan feels she let the family down very badly."

"How?"

"By not loving Jingaluck as much as he does, and not wanting to stay and help work it. Can't blame the poor girl for wanting to get away. There's nothing here for a bright, attractive teenage girl, is there?"

"Her father must have been upset when she left. Did she let them know she was safe, at least? I mean, for all they knew, she could have been abducted."

"Yes, she went to an aunt, on her mother's

side. The woman phoned to let them know. Afterward, I think Caroline sent the odd postcard."

"Does Jonathan resent her for leaving too?"

"I'm sure he does. Especially not coming home for the funeral. He rarely even mentions her. It's as if she ceased to exist for him. My theory is it makes him try twice as hard to make a go of Koolwear. For his dad's sake and for his own family pride as much as for the town."

"You're all very supportive of him."

"Koologong would be dead as a doornail without Jonathan Knight."

"But it takes a cooperative effort. He couldn't do it on his own without all of you working for the same goal."

"True. We're all in it together, sink or swim."

"You're very fortunate it's such a strong community. I envy you all."

"It's a pity you're only passing through. I think you'd fit in perfectly."

Stella laughed. "Oh, no. I'm a city girl. I've enjoyed staying here, and everyone's been wonderfully kind and generous, but as soon as my car's fixed, I'll be leaving. I don't want to wear out my welcome, and I need to go to the bank. By the way, Dan doesn't seem to know much about cars — would Grant take a look at mine for me, do you think? Jonathan said he was the expert."

Judy bit her lower lip and frowned, not seeming to know what to say. "You'll have to ask him," she said eventually. Was Dan easily offended? On short acquaintance, doubtful.

"All right." Stella cast around for another, less problematic topic. "Jonathan wants me to come to the karaoke night at the pub. Do you go?"

Judy's face brightened. "Oh, yes, everyone will be there tonight."

"Why tonight especially?"

"Oh, I didn't mean especially tonight. I meant everyone always goes, and because it's Saturday, everyone will be there. Not especially. No special reason for going tonight."

"I've never been to one."

"It's great fun. Can you sing?" Judy giggled and blushed bright red.

"I can play the piano," said Stella smoothly. "I'd rather do that."

"There's a piano at the pub. Might be fun — a sing-along."

Stella had plinked a few notes on the pub piano on her way past. Casually random keys as if out of idle curiosity, for Leo's benefit if he happened to be in earshot. Not even recognizable as musical notes, poor, neglected old thing.

"Yes."

"But we'd have to convince Leo and everyone else."

"I wouldn't bother," said Stella. "I'm happy to listen."

"You can have a nap this afternoon," said Jonathan as they drove home.

"So can you. You must be tired."

"I can't sleep during the day!"

"Why? Mediterranean people do, and so do most hot-climate people. They take siestas. Very sensible of them."

"I've got work to do."

"You said you'd stay home because it's too hot to go out."

"You're right. It's paperwork." He pulled a face, and Stella laughed.

"Workaholic."

Jonathan grinned at her. "You said you never took holidays either."

Smiling, Stella gazed out the window. It was such a vast country with an enormous sky, harsh and cruel at times but rewarding in its own way and very beautiful. It forged people, this life. Those who survived became strong and resilient. Those who didn't, or couldn't, were either broken, like Jonathan's father, or fled. How would she herself shape up? Too weak and too fond of her creature comforts, too dependent on others.

"Jonathan, thank you for looking after me. I don't know what I would have done if you hadn't offered me a bed for the night."

"Three nights. You'll have to stay Sunday as well."

"Three nights! It's such an imposition." Stella fell silent. How would she survive another two nights in the same house — the rest of today, tonight, and all tomorrow as well — without grabbing him and embarrassing them both again, humiliating herself? In love? Try weak. Needy.

"It's not an imposition," he said quietly. "I'm enjoying your company. Very much."

"Are you? Even though I — I'm — even though, you know?"

Jonathan reached across and took her hand. He squeezed gently, then let it go. He smiled. Stella blinked away a silly tear and looked out the window quickly. When she looked back at him, he was staring straight ahead, but his lips had a slight curve, and he didn't look as tense and tired as before.

Stella was itching to try out her melody on the piano. She waited until Jonathan had shut himself in his office at the far end of the house before opening the lid of the upright and playing a few experimental chords. It didn't sound as bad as she expected. Pianos in these conditions — as proven by Leo's at the pub — unplayed, unmaintained, subject to high temperatures and low humidity, could have everything from keys missing and broken strings to mice nesting in the innards. At the very least she expected it to be hideously out of tune. But it wasn't.

She pulled her loose pages from her pocket and placed her own manuscript paper on the music stand. The one thing she had deliberately brought with her on her flight — blank music paper for composing. Soon she was completely immersed, humming under her breath, stopping and starting, scribbling, erasing. Finally she had something. She stretched her arms over her head, rolled her shoulders to ease the tension from her neck, and played straight through what she'd written. Good! Strong melody, unusual harmonic twists, good hook, nice bridge. A few words were even coming through for the chorus. . . .

"Nice tune," said Jonathan. She nearly fell off the piano stool with surprise. "Sorry — thought you knew I was listening."

"How long have you been there?" she demanded. "I thought you were in your office."

"I was, but I finished half an hour ago. You've been at this for three hours. I didn't know you played the piano."

"Yes. I do." Stella gathered her pages together and closed the lid.

He smiled. "Cup of tea?"

"I'll make it." She made for the door, clutching the new song. *Have to keep him off the subject of music.*

A distant growling startled them both. Stella looked back over her shoulder. "Thunder?"

"Yep. Clouds have been building up all day."

Thunder grumbled and growled again. Closer this time. She dumped her papers onto the nearest chair and followed Jonathan out the front door and down the steps. The sky was deep purple to the northeast. Huge cloudy boulders had piled higher and higher, covering the whole sky now. A hot wind tugged at her hair; whirling dust stung her eyes. The pines by the driveway shivered and sighed. A crack of thunder made her jump. Sheet lightning flared and died.

Clouds raced across the sky. The light had faded to a dramatic, eerie purple glow. The grumbling and roaring continued, but no rain fell. The wind increased as they stood with faces upraised to the turmoil above them. Lightning shafted down in a brilliant arrow, followed immediately by a deafening blast of thunder. The remaining small patches of blue were overtaken by rampaging dark hordes. The temperature plummeted. Stella shivered and rubbed her smarting eyes. A couple of fat drops plopped into the dust at their feet. Two fell on her bare arm.

"It's raining!" She whooped with delight. More and more drops tumbled from the sky, and Jonathan flung his arms wide as if to embrace the storm. Silver streaks pelted down in a stinging deluge, soaking through clothes to the skin in an instant. Laughing, Stella scrambled under the shelter of the veranda and wiped her hands ineffectually across her face. Her blouse stuck to her body, sodden within seconds. Jonathan jumped about like a child, shouting and laughing in the puddles.

"Youch! Hail." He sprinted up the steps to stand beside Stella, dripping and laughing, watching the hailstones bounce on the grass. And it seemed natural and right that his arm should be about her shoulders and her arm should be about his waist.

He looked down at her. "Drowned rat."

"Drowned rat yourself."

He increased the pressure of his arm, drawing her closer, and stared back out at the gray afternoon with a contented smile. The brief flurry of hail had given way to a steady, drenching downpour, gurgling in the gutters and dripping in a heavy curtain from the eaves.

"We need this to last all night. A few days would be good. It's perfect timing. Tops up the falls we've had already."

Stella shivered.

"Better go in and change," he said.

"I'm fine. It's lovely to feel cool. The constant heat was unbearable."

"True, but you're soaked, and so am I."

But he made no move to leave the veranda, and he didn't move his arm. Neither did Stella. She wouldn't move an inch until he did. Until he let his arm slip from her shoulders and removed his body from her embrace. But he didn't. Instead he turned slightly and bent his head to kiss her upturned face, his skin all soft and wet from the rain, and her lips parted in anticipation.

CHAPTER EIGHT

The kiss lasted an instant. Stella's heart stopped beating, her lungs stopped drawing in air, her brain stopped sending signals. Her whole being focused on his lips pressed gently and insistently to hers and his body warm against her. Then it was over. He drew back. His eyes searched hers for a moment before he ran his fingertips across her brow and stroked wet hair from her cheeks.

"You broke the drought," he whispered. "Coming here."

Stella couldn't speak. She wanted to say so much, but no words formed themselves. No words seemed right. He drew a deep breath and let her go. The comfortable coolness turned to the chill of abandonment. She reached for him instinctively, and an inarticulate little noise escaped from her mouth, somewhere between a sob and a cry.

"Jonathan," she managed to breathe. Then she was held fast in his arms as he kissed her the way he'd done the first time. Drops of water fell from his wet hair to her face and trickled down her neck. She didn't care. In his arms she was secure, she was home.

He drew away, gazing into her eyes for a moment before he found her mouth again and stopped her breath with another deep kiss. Stella sighed. She could stay on the veranda in his embrace forever and ever.

But he let her go abruptly and stepped back. "I'm sorry," he rasped. "I'm sorry, Susanna. I can't. We mustn't."

Stella stumbled forward a step as her support was removed. She blinked her eyes open, focused her melted brain. "Why?"

He rubbed his hands over his face, then turned his back to her. "The same reasons," he muttered. "The same as before."

"Not wanting to take advantage of me, you mean? Shouldn't I be the judge? I want to kiss you just as much as you want to kiss me, Jonathan. Don't deny it. Don't pretend."

"I don't. I don't deny it, but it's . . . it's wrong. We don't know each other. It's too quick." He flung the door open and charged into the house.

Stella followed him inside to the living room. "We know we're attracted to each other. Isn't that enough?" she asked, knowing it wasn't nearly enough reason. Not with this man. And not the whole truth. But frustration and disappointment sharpened her tongue.

"No! No, it's not!" He turned to face her then, and the despair on his face almost made her cry. "We have no future, you and I." His voice dropped so much, Stella strained to hear the words over the roar of the rain on the roof. She stepped forward. He stayed where he was, the couch and chairs between them — an ocean of tears away. "If I kiss a woman the way I want to kiss you, I want to see her for more than a few days. I don't want to start something that'll be over before it's begun. But that's all this sort of love could possibly end up being." His voice choked on the last words.

Stella stared at him in wonder. A tear rolled down her cheek. "Do you love me?" she asked, her voice soft, wondering.

Jonathan gazed into her eyes from across the room. "I think I might."

"Oh." Stella collapsed into the nearest chair. She couldn't stand; her legs wouldn't obey her. "Oh," she said again. "I see."

But he didn't know who she was, whom he was loving. How could she tell him now? Had he fallen as fast as she had? Would it make a difference? "But what if I love you too?"

A spark of surprise and perhaps hope flared in his eyes. "You couldn't. You've only just met me. Lust is a totally different thing."

"So have you only just met me."

"But I . . ." Jonathan bit his lip. He shrugged and turned away. "It'd never work. We live completely different lives."

Stella stood up. She'd made the chair wet with her damp clothes. He was right. It would be difficult enough as Susanna Starkey. As Stella Starr — impossible. Hopeless. Continuing this was torturing them both. She couldn't tell him she'd fallen in love as well.

She forced the words out. "Yes. You're right. Better not, then."

"Yes," he said. "Better not."

"Excuse me. I'll have to change." Stella rushed past him and ran to her room, slamming the door behind her. She dragged her wet clothes from her body and fell naked onto the bed. Wrapping the quilt around her, shaking uncontrollably, she buried her face in the pillow so he wouldn't hear the choking, gut-wrenching sobs forcing themselves in an endless stream from the very depths of her soul.

Much later, the phone rang faintly in the distance. After a couple of minutes Jonathan tapped on the door. Stella raised her head a fraction, but he didn't come in. He called, "I have to go out. There's flooding. We have to shift some machinery." He paused. She knew he was still there, waiting for a response. "Susanna?"

"All right," she said. And then, "Take care."

"I don't know how long I'll be."

"I'll be fine."

"All right. See you later."

She heard him clump away down the passage. The back door slammed, and a few moments later the ute's engine started up. Stella lay on her back staring at the ceiling. Rain pattered down in a steady stream. Good, soaking rain — just what they needed. With any luck it would go on all night and tomorrow as well.

She got up and pulled on jeans and a sweatshirt because it was cooler now that the storm had broken. She went to the bathroom and studied her reflection. *Terrible.* Red eyes, swollen, puffy face. Hair a tangled mess. Miserable expression. How could loving and being loved result in this nightmarish apparition? Wasn't being in love supposed to be joyful and uplifting?

"It depends," she said to herself out loud, "whom you choose to fall in love with. And, you being you, have picked the wrong person again."

Her first hit, her teenybopper sensation that burst onto the charts like a skyrocket had been titled "Happy in Love." What did she know about love at that age? Not a lot less than she knew now.

She brushed her hair into order and did the best she could with cold water and makeup and hoped Jonathan would be out long enough for the effects of her crying binge to have worn off. The best to be said about this whole sorry mess was that he didn't realize the full extent of her feelings. That much was obvious. He put her passion down to animal lust, superficial and easily satisfied. But what of his feelings? He said he might be in love. Was he? She'd thought once that if he said he loved, he would mean it. Everything she'd learned about him since had corroborated that opinion. For the first time in her life she'd found a man of integrity who loved her for herself, as a woman and not as Stella Starr, and whom she loved in return.

Stella sighed. Whether he truly loved her or not was irrelevant. He was "righter" about one thing than he'd ever been about anything, if only he knew it. A relationship between them was doomed. Stella Starr just could not carry on a successful and private romance with anyone, let alone someone living the quiet, hardworking life Jonathan did. It would destroy him, and with it their fledgling love. *If* this fragile love could survive the revelation that she'd concealed her real identity and lied to him.

What she ought to do for both their sakes was leave, and as fast as possible. But she couldn't until he came back with the transport.

Stella trailed dismally to the living room and picked up her discarded manuscript. She sat at the piano and played, and the words seemed to flow into her mind and out of her mouth. The melody she had written changed tempo, became a slow ballad instead of an upbeat dance tune.

Please yourself
Sounds so easy.
Please yourself
Can't seem to succeed.
What can I do?
No matter how hard I try
I can't please myself if I can't please you.

Car headlights swept across the windows,

but the engine sounded different than Jonathan's ute. She glanced at the black and gold clock sitting on the mantelpiece. Half-past eight. Visitors? Someone looking for Jonathan? Everyone was supposed to be wowing it up in the pub tonight, although if there was flooding from the downpour, maybe everyone had stayed home.

Stella went to the front door, switched on the light, and stepped out onto the veranda. A woman was dragging a suitcase from the trunk of a battered Toyota. She glanced toward Stella through the sheeting rain, then slammed the lid shut and ran for the house.

Was this the ex-fiancée, Lena? Whoever she was, she appeared to be sure of a welcome, bringing her suitcase. The woman reached the steps and hoisted the sodden bag to shelter. She pushed wet hair from her face and eyes and shook her arms and body like a dog.

"Brrr." She grimaced. "Never expected rain as a homecoming. Who are you?"

Stella stared into a pair of hazel eyes the image of Jonathan's in a face amazingly similar — the same arching eyebrows, the same brow, blonder hair, although this girl's was shaggy and had burgundy streaks. She wore low-cut jeans and a sopping wet long-sleeved T-shirt. Water glistened on the tanned skin of her face and hands.

"Are you Caroline?"

"Sure am. Where's Dad? Does Keith still live here?"

Stella gulped and turned to open the door. "Come in. Come in and dry off. Jonathan's gone out to check something — he's worried about flooding. Keith and Renata have gone to Canberra to a wedding. They'll be back on Wednesday." She held the screen door wide.

"Renata?"

"Keith's wife."

"Hmm." Caroline tilted her head, then picked up her bag and followed Stella indoors. She headed straight for her bedroom. Stella called quickly, "I'm sorry. My things are in there, in your room. I'm — I'm a guest. Jonathan kindly put me up for a few nights. My car's broken down."

Caroline stopped. She put her bag down. Water pooled on the polished floor. "And you are?" She studied Stella through eyes sharp and appraising. Strong, confident. Like her brother.

"Susanna Starkey. I'm from Sydney."

"Hi. Is Dad out with Jon?"

Stella swallowed; She had no choice. "Caroline, I'm sorry. It's not my place to tell you this, but your father . . . well . . . your father died. About six years ago, I think. I'm sorry." She licked her lips, unsure if this was the correct way to deliver such news. She was the wrong person — she knew that much.

Caroline stared, her eyes glassy and hard. "How do you know?"

"Jonathan told me, and so did Doreen in town, at the store."

"Oh." The lips firmed, but she gave no other indication of grief. Shocked perhaps. For a moment stunned. Tired too.

"Come to the kitchen, and I'll make us a cup of tea." Stella placed her hand on Caroline's arm, offering support in a gesture that might or might not be accepted by this strange, strong-willed girl. The cotton sleeve was damp and cold under her fingers. "Maybe you'd rather change your clothes first. Get out of those wet things. Take your bag to your room, and I'll move my stuff."

"No, no, you stay. I'll use the spare room. I suppose there is still a spare room." The voice, erupting harshly from the slender body, startled Stella. The arm was dragged from her grasp.

Stella said, "I don't know. Jonathan uses one as his office. Keith and Renata are in the other wing. I don't know about the other rooms."

"I stopped at the pub on the way through. Why didn't anyone tell me?" A telltale quiver of her lips indicated that the reality of the loss was beginning to sink in. "Eight years. I've been away eight years." She stepped away, breathing hard. Her gaze swung from Stella to a painting on the wall, to her suitcase, back to Stella. She dragged in air, closed her eyes, then opened them. "How did he die?"

"Doreen told me his car hit a train at the level crossing. An accident."

"Ooohh!" Both hands covered her face, and her shoulders heaved convulsively as her voice came in strangled sobs. "I didn't know. Why didn't they tell me? Keith and Jonathan. Why didn't they tell me?"

Stella moved forward with a hand outstretched in tentative comfort. "I don't think anyone knew where you were," she said softly.

Caroline dropped her hands, her eyes bright with tears. She stared at Stella, blinking as though seeing her for the first time. She wiped a hand roughly across her face. "No. I didn't know where I was either."

She picked up her bag and lugged it past Stella's room, through the kitchen, and down another short corridor leading to Jonathan's office. She flung the door open and dumped the bag on the floor. Stella glimpsed a desk with a computer, filing cabinets against a wall, and a divan.

"Caroline, you should use your own bedroom. I can sleep in there."

"I won't be here long." Bitterness twisted her mouth into a painful grimace.

"Neither will I," Stella said. Caroline turned with a puzzled expression. "I'll get you a towel and then make the tea," she added quickly, because Caroline was looking at her with more than puzzlement now. She closed the door, shutting off the examination, and went to the linen cupboard.

Stella heated a can of vegetable soup and made toast as well as the tea. The soup was emitting soft little bubbles of steam when Caroline sat down at the table ten minutes later in black track pants and a floppy, man's shirt.

"Tea," she said. "The cure-all. I used to think my back teeth must be permanently afloat after all the cups of tea I drank out here."

Stella laughed. "It is a bit like that. Hungry? I haven't had dinner." She put the plate of buttered toast on the table.

Caroline picked up a slice and bit off at

least a quarter. "You're Stella Starr, aren't you?" she said casually through the mouthful.

Stella dropped the ladle into the saucepan with a clunk. She dragged in a deep breath and turned to face the girl sitting watching her, chewing with an expectant little smile on her face.

"Yes. But no one knows. Out here. I'm Sue Starkey."

"Escaping? I read about it." Caroline wrinkled her nose. "Can't blame you. It must be horrible being under a microscope the whole time. I'd hate it. All my mistakes scrutinized and discussed by people who don't know me."

"But think they do," said Stella viciously. "And they think they have the right to criticize and comment on the most personal things."

Caroline nodded. "Same reasons I cleared out. Couldn't stand everyone knowing my business and telling me what I should be doing. All those well-meaning old biddies getting in Dad's ear because Mum wasn't around. I hated it. I wanted to be me!"

Stella smiled at Caroline. She knew exactly. "I've loved being Sue. It's wonderful being a normal person, being anonymous. I've been in the spotlight since I was fifteen.

I hardly know who I am away from Stella the star. I'm just beginning to find out."

And making a real hash of it — except Caroline didn't need to know that.

"Jon knows who you are, of course," said Caroline.

Stella ladled soup into two bowls and placed them on the table. "No. No one does. They think I'm Susanna Starkey from Sydney, stuck here because my car broke down. I've no cash to pay Leo for a room, so Jonathan offered me a bed. Very kind of him." She stopped.

Caroline was staring at her in amazement. "Of course Jon knows who you are. He'd recognize you in a second!" she cried. "He's drooled over you since he was seventeen, and you had your first hit. What was it?"

"Happy in Love." She could barely force out the name. What a joke the title was now.

"Right 'Happy in Love.' He's got all your albums. He must be beside himself. He adores you." She added, after swallowing a mouthful of toast, "Or he used to when I saw him last. Eight years ago."

"He never said," whispered Stella. She met Caroline's gaze, so like Jonathan's it made her heart turn over. "Why wouldn't he say?"

Caroline ran her tongue over her lips.

"Maybe he didn't want to upset you if you wanted to be anonymous." She tilted her head, frowning. Shrugged. "Maybe he had other reasons. Leo would've put you up at the pub. He'd take a credit card for sure. Jonathan could easily have driven you into Walgett or Bourke to a bank if he wanted to be so helpful."

"That's what I suggested, but he said he was too busy, with Keith away." Stella laid down her spoon, a cold, hard lump forming in her belly.

Caroline spooned up more soup in silence.

"He lied to me. They all did," said Stella eventually. "I never thought he'd lie. I thought . . ."

"Jon looks out for himself and this property, full stop." Caroline scraped her spoon around the bowl.

Stella's appetite had shriveled into the tight little knot of her stomach. "They think he's wonderful in town. He's their savior with his cotton company."

"Yeah, Koolwear," said Caroline. "It was just getting going when I left. He was still at Uni finishing his degree, and he'd come home for the holidays full of talk about this brilliant idea. Keith was here running sheep like Dad and Grandpop. Jon'd go around badgering all the farmers. Nag, nag, nag.

Drove me mad. I hated him for it. He never for one minute doubted that anyone would be as keen as he was about the thing. Me included. He never listened to me when I told him I had other plans. No one ever listened to me."

"What did you want to do?" The vehemence and bitterness of Caroline's words jolted Stella out of her own misery.

"Art. But that was a waste of time to him and Dad. I've just finished my own degree — in graphic design."

"Congratulations." She'd barely scraped through high school in between recording and concert tours. "It must have been hard doing it all by yourself."

"Yes. I worked to earn every penny to pay for it. Thing was, I could have helped Jon at the start. If he'd helped me a bit. If he'd been less obsessed with wretched Koolwear and more interested in his little sister. I could have helped with advertising and design and stuff. I would've liked that."

They sat in silence. Caroline rose and poured the remains of the soup into her bowl, then took another piece of toast. She said softly with her back turned, "I keep expecting Dad to come in."

"I'm sorry."

"Not your fault, our family problems."

She gave Stella a brittle smile as she sat down.

"Why did you come back? Now, I mean."

"I wanted to show Dad and Jon I wasn't the waste of time and space they thought I was."

"I don't think . . ."

"You don't know," snapped Caroline. Then she grimaced. "Sorry. I forgot who you are. Sorry."

"Don't! Don't apologize." Stella slammed her hand on the table. "That's what I mean. I want to be a person, not a celebrity — as if it makes me somehow different. Yell at me, tell me I'm a pain. I want to be Sue, a woman."

"But you can't be," said Caroline, unperturbed by the explosion. "You can't just pretend Stella Starr doesn't exist. She's part of you. You're her. You can't put a lid on your creative side and hope it stays on. I know firsthand, believe me."

Stella stared at her hand on the table. "No, you're right. I have to go back. I was planning to leave as soon as possible, but I need a ride into town."

"Tonight?"

Stella nodded.

"I can take you."

"No, I'll wait for Jonathan, I think. There

are some things to say."

Caroline said shrewdly, "Has he been his usual obnoxious self? Is that why you want to leave?"

Stella's cheeks warmed uncomfortably. "Not really. He's been very generous. It's not . . . It's . . ." She bit her hp. "I just want to know why." Unbearably conscious of Caroline's gaze, she pushed back her chair and stood up. She had to get away, think this through alone. Regroup. "Excuse me."

Stella sat on her bed, staring at the floor. Why would Jonathan pretend he didn't know who she was? To help keep her secret? Maybe, but he could still tell her in private, and they could keep the secret together, especially if what he'd told her was true. But was it? Might he really be in love with her?

Not likely. If what Caroline said was true, and she had no reason to doubt her, Jonathan was just another besotted fan eager to get his paws on Stella Starr. And he had. She'd made it very easy for him. Stella's face and necked burned with the shame of it. She put her hands up to her scorching cheeks in horror. He knew! All the time he was flirting and offering her dinner as a kindly gesture, asking about her life, he knew. When she kissed him, she must have made his day. All the time he was laughing at her, chortling to himself about having Stella Starr in his house. And telling his mates! Good grief! If Jonathan knew, they all knew. Those Koologong people stuck as close as Xavier to his accountant.

How could she face any of them? They'd think she was out of her mind, swanning around pretending to be an ordinary girl. Some sort of loony celebrity slumming it in the outback. No wonder Judy had carried on the way she did. So stupid not to have put two and two together. Judy's reaction had been all too familiar, if she'd been half awake and not enjoying herself so much.

Jonathan drove down the muddy track, gripping the wheel to keep control as the ute slipped and slid around the curves. He had to check the river level. Barry McRae had reported floodwaters coming down from higher upstream. A low-lying bridge connected two of the cotton fields. If it went under, Grant's equipment in sheds close to the riverbank would be isolated and in danger. It all had to be moved. He met Grant and his boys at the sheds, and they got to work.

Physical labor in unpleasant conditions —

just what he needed to take his mind off Stella. Except she wouldn't get out of his head. He wanted her so much, it hurt. Deep inside, deeper than his brain, deeper than his heart, right down in the depths of his soul. His whole being cried out for her, and he had no idea how he would survive without her. It was as if his whole life had been spent waiting for her.

Jonathan decided, as he drove the gigantic roaring tractors and harvesters to higher ground, when he got home he'd go straight to Stella and tell her exactly how he felt. Wake her up if necessary. He'd tell her he knew who she was and was prepared to do anything she wanted so they could be together. Anything. It might not be a wise move to tell her why he hadn't let on he knew her identity. Let her think he was merely keeping her secret for her. The important thing was that she know he loved her. Really loved her, not as a fan idolizes a fantasy, but as a man loves a woman.

Then she could decide whether she loved him the same way. It felt very much to him during their rain-soaked kiss on the veranda as though she were similarly inclined. But she could be just a passionate woman. Could be? She was. Marvelously so. But what did he know about celebrities and their habits? What was the norm for the rich and famous?

On the way back, late, no visibility due to pouring rain, treacherous mud and vast new potholes, Jonathan swung past the house and continued down to the ford on the driveway. Just as he'd suspected, a rushing torrent of muddy, swirling water cut them off from easy access to town. They could go the long way via Grant's, but chances were, the low bridge would be under by now too. He grinned with satisfaction. He and Stella were cut off for a day at least, and if the rain kept on, maybe two or more. Plenty of time to get their feelings sorted out. And if all went well . . . There wasn't much outside work to be done in the wet; they'd have to stay indoors.

Lights were on in the house, glinting yellow through the sheets of rain and the blackness of the night. She'd either stayed up or left a welcoming light on. He drove into the garage, hoisted an old umbrella, and ran for the house, boots, socks, and trousers already soaked by the earlier activity. What would she be doing? Listening to music? Composing, maybe? Worrying about him? She'd called, "Take care," with her voice sounding young and tentative. She needed looking after, his Stella. She was the one who needed care.

He dragged off his boots, peeled off the wet, muddy socks, and left them in the laundry, then padded through the kitchen to his bedroom for dry jeans, socks, and a sweater. After a quick wash, he went to find her. In the living room. The murmur of voices. Listening to the radio or watching TV. Jonathan smiled in anticipation, but his mouth froze as two faces turned toward him.

"Hello, Jon."

"Carrie?"

His gaze flew to Stella, watching with a blank expression. She looked aloof, distant. Angry? Why? No time to ponder or analyze. Carrie stood up. She'd grown into a woman. A lovely woman, he registered through his total astonishment. A self-confident young woman looking at him with the old contempt and the sarcastic half smile that used to make him grind his teeth.

"You're looking good," she said.

"So are you. You look great." He stepped forward uncertainly with an arm extended. He smiled. His little sister. Home at last. "I'm so glad —" His voice broke; he stopped. He swallowed.

Carrie studied him for a moment. Her face crumpled. "Stella told me about Dad."

Her voice cracked. She stumbled awkwardly into his arms, and he clutched her to him as she sobbed into his shoulder.

They clung together for what seemed an eternity, murmuring apologies, nothings; then Carrie pulled away and groped for a tissue. Not finding one, she flung Stella a cryptic glance and left the room. Jonathan cleared his throat. He turned away to sit down, but something she'd said lodged in his brain. *Stella* had told her? His attention whipped to Stella, who'd sat silent and unmoving through their reunion. Now her eyes were moist, her demeanor less intimidating.

"I haven't seen her for eight years," he said.

"I know."

"How long has she been here?"

Stella glanced at the clock. "Four hours. Plenty of time."

"For what?"

"Talking."

Talking. Time for some more. He had to say it, get it in first before the inevitable explosion. Jonathan rose and sat next to her on the couch. Her face swung toward him, cool, expressionless. Distant.

"I love you," he said.

She blinked. "Me? And exactly who am I,

Jonathan?"

His heart contracted, missing a couple of beats. Carrie! Carrie had recognized her, of course. Some talk they must have had. Nothing for it; he had to make her understand.

"You, the woman sitting next to me. The woman I kissed. The woman I want to kiss again right now. The woman who kissed me. The woman I love with all my heart."

A flush stained her cheeks. She dropped her gaze for an instant but said coldly, "And what's her name?" She looked up.

Jonathan plunged deep into her eyes. She met his gaze, hers unwavering with a flinty hardness he'd never seen before.

"I don't care what her name is," he said softly, intently.

"You knew, didn't you?" she rasped. "You lied to me the whole time. You pretended, you lied, and you made me look a complete fool. It must have been such a riot. Such a joke."

The muscles in her cheeks clenched; her jaw worked as she strove to keep control.

But she was wrong. Terribly wrong. "No." He rapped the word out like a gunshot. "Never. I never thought you were a joke."

"Why did you do it?" Barely above a whisper. "Why? You knew I could pay Leo.

You must have known. I saw you muttering together, looking guilty — plotting. Why did you insist on bringing me out here? Did you think you could seduce me? Stella Starr? What a coup."

She'd turned her face away, but he knew there were tears hovering. His fingers itched to stroke the soft line of her cheek, caress the hurt from her, but he needed words. The right words.

"But I didn't, did I?" he asked just as softly. "I wanted to. You know exactly how much I wanted to, and so did you. At first I thought you were out for a good time at my expense. A woman like you couldn't possibly be attracted to a man like me for long." He looked down at her hands, fingers white from gripping each other so tightly in her lap, revealing the tension suffusing her body. "I wanted to tell you. . . ." She was watching his face now, and he stared into her eyes again, willing her to understand, to believe him. "What I said to you was true. I knew what you'd been through, the divorce, the publicity. You were too vulnerable."

"So you changed your mind. Your scruples got the better of you at the last minute."

"No."

Stella pounced. Her voice was strong, demanding all of a sudden. "What was it, then?" She unclenched her fingers, then leaned forward a fraction, as though trying to draw an answer from him. A proper answer, one she could believe. One she could trust.

Jonathan took her hands, the softness of her palms against his rough, work-worn skin. He remembered the way they'd stroked his cheek, his neck, gripped his body when she kissed him. And he'd stopped her. She didn't understand why at the time, and she didn't believe him now. He lifted her hands and kissed them with all the gentleness of his love.

"I love you, Susanna. Never forget that. It's important."

The hard expression melted to something softer, gender. "Why did you want me to stay in Koologong so badly? Tell me, Jonathan."

Carrie's voice came from the doorway. Sad, resigned. "It's got something to do with his company, hasn't it, Jon? You thought you could get her to back you in some way."

The softness drained from Stella's eyes, the rich brown all at once dull and lifeless. "Is she right?" The words were a mere whisper of sound. She seemed to have shrunk within herself. Her hands were as cold as death in his before she wrenched them from his grasp. "Don't lie to me anymore, please."

He nodded. The truth. The whole truth. He owed her that now. Now that he'd destroyed her fragile confidence so comprehensively. And with it her trust in him and any possibility of her love. Perhaps the truth would salvage something from this wreckage and devastation he'd caused.

"I recognized you straightaway. Of course I did. I've adored you since I was seventeen. How could I not know you? I didn't *really* know you, though. I only knew the public persona, the star. I thought if I could get you to stay long enough in Koologong, you'd see what a fantastic place it is and what a great product we have. I wanted you to be our model. Miss Koolwear. To help the business and the town."

Stella stared at him, horror-struck. "You wanted to use me."

"No, I wanted . . ."

"You did. You're like all the others. Everyone wants a piece of Stella Starr."

"You haven't changed at all," said Caroline. "Still the same self-centered bully, forcing people to do what you want."

"Shut up!" he shouted at her, leaning so casually against the door frame, sneering in the familiar, mocking way. "You haven't changed either. You've only been back a few hours, and already you're causing trouble."

"Don't shout at Caroline," hissed Stella. "She didn't cause this. You did."

He'd lost. Nothing salvageable at all. A total disaster with fire and brimstone raining down on all sides. Jonathan turned his anger and distress back on Stella.

"And you didn't? You lied pretty thoroughly too, you know, Susanna Starkey who works in a music shop."

Stella looked at Caroline. "You offered me a ride into town?" Distant, aloof, a star.

"You want to leave now?" Caroline frowned, doubt evident in her tone. She glanced at her brother. Two against one. Stella didn't belong here.

"Too right I do." She spun back to Jonathan. "I don't think Leo will insist on cash anymore, do you? You manipulating so-and-so."

She stalked to the door. "And by the way, if you want me to be Miss Koolwear, send a proposal to my manager, and he'll put it in the pile with all the other begging letters. I doubt whether you could afford me, though."

Jonathan clenched his fists by his sides. He took a deep breath and said with casual nonchalance through gritted teeth, "The ford's flooded. You can't leave. We're all stuck with each other."

CHAPTER NINE

"I'm going to bed." Caroline backed out of the room hastily.

"Me too," said Stella.

"Susanna." The sharpness in his voice made her pause. She couldn't bear to turn and face him — she'd cry, was only just standing up as it was. The rush of adrenaline-fueled rage had subsided, leaving her weak and trembling at the enormity of his betrayal.

He came closer but didn't touch her. He stood behind her. His voice was husky now, and the words emerged as though his throat was raw and painful. "I'm sorry. It seemed like a good idea at the time. Before I got to know you better. I thought you'd be a spoiled, rich . . . but now . . . I was wrong. You're every bit as perfect as I always imagined you'd be."

"Yes, well, that's what they all say. Stella's so obliging, such a good sport. Ask Stella, she's sure to do it. Everybody loves Stella. Perfectly lovely Stella," she said to the empty doorway and the darkened hall. Her voice shook. She clamped her lips tightly together, staring at the painting on the opposite wall, dimly visible in the gloom — gum trees and scattered sheep. She could feel him there behind her, longed to fall back into his arms and trust his words, trust him to care for her. But she couldn't. "Everybody wants something. Everybody wants a piece of Stella."

"I don't want you to do anything! I want *you*. I fell in love with Susanna. Deeply in love."

"Susanna doesn't exist. I invented her, and now she's gone. She was a complete failure." The bitterness burned acidly in her mouth. "And, like you said, there's no future for you and a city girl — or Stella. Especially not now."

"I love you. We can find a way to make it work." His voice was low and intense in her ear. "You said what if you loved me. Do you?"

Stella turned slowly to face him then. "I thought I did, Jonathan. I thought I'd fallen in love for the first time in my life. I felt . . ." She cast about for the right word, couldn't find it, settled for a weaker one. ". . . different. But now I see I can't ever have that kind of true love with someone, because I'll never truly know if it's me or Stella Starr he's loving." A warped smile contorted her lips. "And what he can get from her. I've done that, Jonathan. I married and divorced it." Her eyes narrowed as she studied him, trying to read the truth behind the words. She tried in vain to find something telling her this was real, this man would be the special one. "How do I know this will be different when it's started out exactly the same way? Deception and lies. Worse. At least Mark was upfront about liking the lifestyle and what it provided. He just ultimately preferred another woman to me. And I don't trust my own feelings anymore either, I've made too many mistakes. And mine are all public ones, remember."

"I don't know what else to say to you," he said helplessly.

Stella gazed into his face, memorizing the tiny lines around his mouth, the brown flecks staining the deep green of his eyes, the lock of sandy hair falling across his brow, the tanned skin, and the prickle of stubble emerging from the unshaven jaw. How could she have been so wrong about him? How could she love someone so much and make such a fundamental mistake, miss such a gigantic lie?

"Say good-bye," she suggested.

"No!"

He gripped her shoulders with strong fingers. She winced but didn't struggle. Instead her eyes filled with tears, and he wrapped his arms around her with a groan of despair, a drowning man clutching at salvation.

She didn't resist. She rested her head against his chest and wished she could stay there forever. Safe, secure, protected from the world, protected from herself. But she didn't put her arms around him. She couldn't. They hung limply by her sides as she let him hold her. It was an illusion, this refuge from the world. Loving Jonathan was a fantasy. His everlasting love, which he pronounced so definitively, was an illusion as well. What else would, or could, he think, faced with his idol so suddenly and unexpectedly? All his Christmases come at once. Grab her with both hands. Of course he'd imagine he was in love. Like all the rest of them.

"I'll love you forever," he said, the words coming in uneven, broken clumps. "I'll love you whether you're Stella Starr or whether you're Sue Starkey. I'll love you even if you never sing another note or sell another CD.

I don't care. I love you, and I'll be here waiting for you."

Stella pulled away from his embrace. "I wouldn't be much use to you as Miss Koolwear then, would I?" She clamped her teeth together to prevent her lips from trembling.

"I don't care. It was a stupid, irrational, spur-of-the-moment idea, and it was wrong."

He could see it now, anyone could see it now, but he'd used her and manipulated her and lied, and it hurt. Hurt more than she'd ever been hurt before. And by the one man she'd thought was honest and straightforward, thought had integrity, and had admired even before she fell in love with him. Because, despite it all, she did love him. She couldn't turn the love off as easily as she denied it to him. But just how much did he think he loved her? How much did he really care about Koolwear?

"Would you give up Koolwear and Jingaluck to follow me and my career?"

Jonathan frowned down at her. "But wasn't that the whole point of becoming Susanna? You wanted to change your life?"

"Partly."

Jonathan reached for her again, but Stella stepped back quickly. "I love to sing, Jonathan. I'll never give that up. Not for anyone.

223

I couldn't live without music."

"I never said I —"

"But you would. You'd get sick of it. Of me. There's not much else to me, I've discovered. I don't know anything. I barely scraped through high school."

"Have you ever tried something else?"

Stella stared at him. She had her answer. He didn't understand, couldn't understand the artistic drive that was as much a part of her as the air she breathed and the blood flowing through her veins. Jonathan hadn't recognized the same compulsion in his sister, and she'd escaped to survive. Left her home and family. He wouldn't give up anything for Stella. His love had limits. They were defined by the Jingaluck boundary fences.

"I'll call Xavier in the morning, and he'll organize a plane for me. Good night Jonathan. Thanks for letting me stay."

Jonathan opened his mouth to speak, but Stella turned her back and fled to the sanctuary of her room, where she thanked heaven she'd never blurted out the depth of her own feelings to him.

Xavier was beside himself with joy the next morning on the other end of the phone. First came relief that his star sounded sane, safe, healthy, and ready to resume work. He positively gushed. Stella pictured his pudgy face beaming with satisfaction at the publicity prospects. He might have even danced a little jig when he heard her voice. Dollar signs must have flashed before his eyes as he figured where best to sell exclusive rights to her story — which TV channel, which magazine, which reporter.

"Keep it quiet where I've been, Xavier. I don't want any of these people bothered."

"Of course, darling. As far as anyone who counts knows, you've been off on a little holiday at a secret location. I'll send Darrell to get you. He'll be there this afternoon. Might have to use a helicopter to reach the property, then fly out from a bigger town with an airstrip. Some interesting offers have come in while you've been finding yourself. And some very exciting news, which I'll tell you when you get back to civilization. I'm so glad you're coming home. I've missed you, Stella."

"Thanks, Xavier." He really nearly sounded sincere. But that wasn't fair. She knew she was more than just a big earner and a meal ticket to Xavier. After her mother had faded into her twilight world, he'd cared for her in his own inimitable fashion, hiring companions and teachers when she was still young enough to need them. He was a canny businessman, and she trusted him. He made sure she wasn't exploited and made sure she invested her earnings wisely. And it was those earnings that secured good care for her mother. But he always had an eye on the next rung of the ladder — "Onward and Upward" was his motto. He forgot, most of the time, that she was a young woman and not a singing, dancing machine.

"There's a charity show on Friday. They'd love you to appear — they requested 'Happy in Love.' I know you're not keen on doing the old stuff, but it'd be a marvelous way of coming back — show everyone you're still on top of things." His tactful way of saying, "prove you haven't lost your marbles or turned to drugs."

Stella closed her eyes. She'd started out on this self-finding mission determined to please herself. Be selfish for the first time in her life. Everyone around her pleased themselves at her expense.

She'd loved her husband and wanted to please him. He'd pleased himself. Mark was good at it. Much better than she was. He'd pleased himself right out the door and into the bed of another woman. A groundswell of rage began to build deep inside her as she realized just how many times she'd said yes when inside she screamed no.

She didn't want to do a charity gig. She'd do others one day, but not this one.

"No," she said as an experiment, not really expecting it to work. She hadn't used the word much to Xavier.

"But, darling! Is it the song? Choose another one."

It was the song, but not just the song. "No, Xavier. No, no, and no." So easy! Stella smiled at the shocked silence. Her rising anger subsided like milk going off the boil, sinking back into the pan moments before it could make a mess everywhere.

"You don't mean it." He'd be evaluating and justifying her reaction to himself. She almost literally heard his brain clicking and whirring as it computed this unheard-of response. "It's too soon. I shouldn't have asked. Forgive me. Think about it."

"No," she said, getting the hang of this selfishness business. All you had to do was be firm and unwavering leaving no room for leverage by the other person.

"It's for animals."

That was an underhanded maneuver. Xavier was sneaky and persistent. That's why he was such a good manager. That and greed.

"Sick animals," he added.

"No." She bit her lip, grimacing and holding her breath.

"All right, darling. Take care. Love you," he said in the voice that meant he hadn't given up but was prepared to let things be for the moment. He'd treated her the same way at the age of fifteen. Like a biddable, six-year-old child. Which was exactly how she'd always acted. Eager to please. Wanting to be liked.

The Stella who arrived in Sydney tonight would not be the Stella who had left two weeks ago. This Stella was strong. A new woman. At least on the outside.

She replaced the phone in its cradle. The house was quiet. She didn't know where Jonathan was. He might have gone out earlier, but she hadn't heard noises from the bathroom. She imagined, as it was seven-thirty, that Caroline was asleep. At least someone had been able to sleep. She certainly hadn't, and she'd bet her last cent Jonathan hadn't either.

Filling the kettle to make tea, she stared out the window at the terrace where they'd had the barbecue. The wet tiles were slick and shiny, but the rain had stopped overnight. Lancelot ambled across the tiles and stopped to lap at a puddle. The pool water lay gray and uninviting, miserably reflecting the low-hanging clouds. More rain coming.

The paddocks looked beautiful in the rain-washed, soft, morning light. Little wisps of steamy cloud vapor twined around the tree trunks, the dry earth and previously dusty, tired leaves now refreshed and sparkling clean. A few magpies caroled in the distance, but nothing else disturbed the quiet and the peace. Too wet for the cicada chorus. No kangaroos about.

Stella took her mug of tea outside to sit on the front veranda on the swinging seat. The scent of wet eucalyptus hung heavy in the air, mingling with the perfume of the roses. So beautiful. Lancelot wandered around the corner and came to lie at her feet. What would it be like to live out here? Would she get bored? Never. There was always something to do on a working property, and this one had the added complication of the business.

Which she knew nothing about. She'd told Jonathan the truth. She was a musician. She knew nothing else, could do nothing else, wanted to do nothing else, and never had. She was born to sing, and if singing was taken away from her, she'd cease to exist.

Try something else, he'd said. He thought she could switch occupations the way he'd switched crops on Jingaluck. Turn from unproductive sheep, cattle, or wheat to cotton. He'd convinced his neighbors, and they'd all done pretty well so far. But it wasn't the same for her. And when it came to the crunch, he wouldn't give up farming, because he felt the same way about the land as she did about music. The way he'd spoken over their first dinner that night in the pub had told her so.

Stalemate.

"Daydreams, Lancelot." He thumped his tail twice on the wooden veranda. "I don't belong here."

And it was true even if they had had no bitter words between them, no deceit, and no gaping chasm filled with shattered trust and avowals of love.

Stella and Caroline walked down to look at the flooded ford later in the morning. Jonathan must have risen earlier than Stella and disappeared somewhere on the property in the ute, because it was gone from the garage when Caroline checked. Lancelot padded along with them, sniffing at interesting smells enhanced by the wet as he went.

"Are you staying long?" asked Stella.

Caroline smiled cheerfully this morning. Striding along with a confident tread, she gazed about, drinking in the sight of the trees and the paddocks, smiling at the screeching cockatoos, patting Lancelot when he came close enough.

"I really want to stay permanently — never mind what I said last night. I was tired and upset about Dad. Despite all the frantic panic to get away from here, I missed it when I got to the city. I guess I'm a country girl at heart."

"Where did you go? Your dad must have been sick with worry."

"I planned everything. I'm not an idiot. I stayed with my aunt on my mother's side. She rang Dad, saying I was safe, but she didn't give an address or a contact." Caroline laughed softly. "On pain of death. Not that she ever liked Dad much."

They walked a few paces in silence. The track was slippery, brown puddles creating an obstacle course. Mud caked their shoes soon after they started out. Caroline spread her arms and took deep, cleansing breaths.

"I just love the fresh, clean air out here, especially after rain. You'll notice the pollution when you go back."

"I know," said Stella. "I sat on the veranda earlier. It's beautiful, and I can see how it becomes a part of you."

"Will you sort things out with Jon before

you go? I didn't mean to butt in last night. I'm sorry if I upset you."

"It's better I know." Stella glanced sideways at her companion. Caroline's face in profile was achingly similar to Jonathan's. How could he have done it to her? Was he going to tell her he knew who she was? Ever? And what did he think he would say when it came to crunch time? "We've nothing left to say to each other," she said. "Sometimes it's best to just cut your losses and leave it."

Caroline kept her mouth shut, but judging by the set of her lips and her skeptical expression, she obviously didn't think this was an accurate assessment.

"Will *you* sort things out with him?" Stella countered the unspoken thought.

"Oh, yes," Caroline said blithely. "Jon and I love each other. We know that. He's just a monumental pain in the neck most of the time. I can handle him now, though. I've learned a thing or two since I was seventeen. And I need a job. I've got skills to offer, and I'm very good at what I do."

"I wish I had."

Caroline gave a shout of laughter. "You're kidding. Stella Starr wishing she had skills to offer? As if."

She smiled. "No. I wish I'd learned something else since I was seventeen."

"Stella, you have. You've just learned different things. You've traveled the world, you've performed in front of crowds of thousands, you've met all sorts of people. . . ." She waved her arms around dramatically. "You know heaps about music and making people feel good."

"I missed out on an adolescence. When my school friends were going to parties and having their first kisses, or playing netball and swapping clothes, I was recording songs and doing concert tours. I have no idea how to recognize real love or even friendship. From anyone, man or woman. I don't know how to get someone to love me for who I am."

"Nobody learns that. You either meet the right guy, or you don't."

"But how do you know?"

"Don't ask me," said Caroline. "If I knew, I wouldn't be separated and pregnant."

"Pregnant?" Stella stopped abruptly.

Caroline nodded. She peeked at Stella from behind her shaggy mop of hair. "That's why I came home. And . . ."

"The father? I mean, your husband? Where . . ."

"He doesn't know."

"How long were you married?" Must have

been an even more spectacular failure than her own disaster.

"About five minutes, but I don't think I want to talk about it." Caroline strode on toward the ford visible through the trees, a muddy, roaring torrent.

"I'd love to be pregnant," Stella said to her departing back.

"I'll swap you." Caroline slowed her pace.

"What a pair we are." Stella slipped her arm through Caroline's. "I'll help any way I can — if you need money or somewhere to stay — you know?"

"You mean if Jon throws me out?"

Stella grimaced. "He won't, will he?"

"No, I don't think so. As I said before, we basically love each other, and we're family. Jon's big on family."

"That's why he was so upset when you left, I think," said Stella. "He sounded very bitter when I asked about you. Will you be all right, really?"

"Yep. I'll behave myself, and he'll be pleased there's an heir to the family fortune on its way. Unless Keith has kids?"

"No. Renata will be thrilled, I think. She's very welcoming."

"Hope so."

"Does Jonathan like children?"

Caroline shrugged. "Don't know. He

hasn't ever said he doesn't."

They looked at the wildly flowing water for a few minutes. No hope of a vehicle crossing in safety.

Caroline said, "Stella, I don't know what's been happening between you two, but I know one thing for certain — Jon would never say he loved you to get at your money. He wouldn't have even taken it into consideration. He would've been thinking purely of promoting Koolwear. And you must admit, he had a point. But he wouldn't tell you he loved you for that reason, either. I know him well enough to know that for certain."

Stella swallowed through a tight knot in her throat and nodded. "I thought exactly the same thing when I first met him. I distinctly remember thinking that if this man says he loves someone, he'll mean it."

"Well then . . ."

"Well, then, nothing."

Caroline squeezed Stella's arm. "I'm sorry. I guess I'm assuming you feel the same way about him."

"I've only known him a few days. He has an advantage. All my fans know more about me than I do."

Caroline cried out in dismay, "Oh, Stella, Jon's not like that! I think he honestly does love you. He was never a love 'em and leave 'em guy. He's always been cautious with women, despite the arrogant, overconfident attitude he's got, I can't see he'd change so fundamentally in the time I've been away." She threw Stella a grin. "Everything else about him seems depressingly the same."

They strolled back up the gentle slope away from the raging floodwater. Caroline whistled to Lancelot, and he came with muddy paws and wet coat to run along beside them. She said, "Jonathan can't have loved anyone as much before you, or he'd be married by now. If he sets his heart on something, he goes all out for it."

"Maybe he does love me, but how could anything work between us? Tell me, Caroline. It wouldn't be parents or distance coming between us, but photographers and fans and all the hoo-ha that goes with celebrity. You've seen what happens to me. It's impossible. I wouldn't subject him to it." Stella's voice cracked when she added, "Even if I did . . . love him."

Stella slogged along the slippery, gooey track toward the house with Caroline and Lancelot trailing behind.

The red ute was back, but when the two women removed their muddy shoes at the laundry door and entered the house in socks, they discovered that Jonathan had sequestered himself in the study with the door shut. Stella went to her room to pack her few things. Caroline leaned in the doorway watching.

"When are you leaving?"

"Not sure, exactly. Xavier's organized a plane or a helicopter. Sometime this afternoon."

"Wow." Caroline's eyes widened at such blatant evidence of Stella's wealth.

"I'll give you my home address and private number. Please don't give them to anyone else." She scribbled her details on a piece of manuscript paper.

"Of course I won't!"

Stella flicked a smile on and off. "Call me if you need to. Promise?"

"Yes."

She clicked her red suitcase closed and lifted it off the bed. "You should move your things in here now. I'm sorry I pinched your room."

"Don't be," said Caroline. "I think I need to lie down. I get really tired halfway through the day."

"I'll find clean linen."

"No, no. Don't bother. I'll do it later." She caught the look on Stella's face, interpreted it accurately, and added hastily, "I need to lie down right away."

Stella carried her case to the door. "I'll wake you for lunch."

"Thanks." Caroline sat down on the bed and gazed around. "It looks exactly the same as when I left."

"They probably kept it hoping you'd come home. You're lucky to have such a wonderful place to come back to." She closed the door before Caroline could see the tears welling in her eyes.

Stella left her suitcase by the front door and went to the living room. Rain fell again. Soft and steady now without the passion and drama of yesterday. She lay back on the couch against the cushions stacked at one end and tucked her feet under her, listening to the soothing cadence of falling water. Caroline was very lucky to have this home to retreat to, this bolt-hole, this safe place to hide when life became too tough for a young woman. Particularly one expecting a baby without the father's support.

Stella's only bolt-hole was her charade as Susanna, and now that that flimsy cover had been ripped away, she had no option but to return to work, to Xavier. Let him take care of things as he always had. She had no one else. Her mother was in her own secret little world, and her one aunt had passed away years ago. Of her father's relatives she knew very little. An uncle somewhere, maybe a few cousins, but none had ever contacted her, which was surprising, given her celebrity. They either didn't know or didn't care. Or both. What she had of family amounted to nothing, because her dear mum didn't know who her only child was anymore.

She didn't even have a home. She had the penthouse in Sydney but hadn't lived there much. Mark had chosen it, but he took the apartment in LA in the settlement. Neither place was a home. Not like Jingaluck.

Caroline's child would grow up loved and happy here, part of a strong, supportive community. She was right to come back, certain of a welcome, however difficult at first, and however humbling the experience. But perhaps Caroline's husband would come looking for her, and they could start again. They must have had something, to take such a big step as marriage. She and Mark had been in love at first. Caroline was impulsive, though. Far more so than Stella. Love was a difficult thing to catch hold of. Something slippery and intangible. A fantasy?

Someone entered the room. She looked up. Jonathan. She met his gaze but couldn't speak. She had nothing to say to him that would make any more sense than what had already been said. Tired lines furrowed his cheeks; the skin about his eyes was pale. An unaccustomed air of defeat radiated from him as he moved to squat by the couch.

"Stella, please understand that what I did had nothing to do with you as a person, but everything to do with you as an image. Your public image."

"I understand perfectly, Jonathan. Everyone sees me as an image and not a person." She gave a short, mirthless laugh. "I understand now why Judy stayed in the bathroom with me. I thought it was because she was a bit simpleminded. I'm so dense. She's like everyone else — amazed to see that Stella Starr actually had to wash her hands and use the loo."

"I'm sorry. What else can I say?" He rubbed his palms across his brow and cheeks, let his hands drop to his thighs, then pushed to his feet and dropped into an armchair.

"Look after Caroline," she said.

He glanced at her sharply. "Why? Is she in trouble?"

"Not really. I don't think so. She should be all right, now that she's home." Her breath caught on the last word, and she looked down quickly. He couldn't have any idea how she longed for a home, a proper one with people who loved her for herself, faults and all.

"I'm glad she's back," he said softly. "Keith will be too. And Renata. They haven't met." She knew, then, he would welcome the baby. Caroline was right about him. He treasured his small family unit. He was a good man.

"Caroline's a lovely person. I feel I could . . . we . . ." Stella jumped up. "I'll make lunch. Someone should be here for me soon." Never had she felt more like an outsider, an interloper, and never felt more desperately that she wanted to belong. But she had to keep up her defenses. Jonathan had no idea what he would be in for — chaos would ensue. His life would become a public spectacle.

"I'll make a Spanish omelet, shall I?"

He followed her to the kitchen. Occasionally she moved near him to reach for a knife or a bowl, or he brushed against her as he took down plates from a shelf. Every touch scorched her to the soul, every accidental linking of eyes, quickly averted, destroyed another brick in her wall of defense. He did nothing to alleviate the tension, or perhaps he didn't feel it as acutely as she did.

Stella's lungs tightened with every breath

until she was taking in teaspoonfuls of air and shaking so much that the spatula rattled against the side of the frying pan. She quickly switched off the heat.

"I'll wake Caroline," she murmured, and she made to push past him, standing at the counter buttering toast. He dropped the knife with a clatter, reached out an arm, and drew her hard against him. For a split second he gazed into her eyes, then the remaining bricks in her tottery wall came crashing down as he kissed her. But even as she closed her eyes and clutched him to her in a last desperate attempt to shut out reality, her mind knew it was hopeless. She allowed her body to absorb every detail of the embrace, to memorize every reaction from every nerve ending in every part of her, because when Jonathan kissed her, she came alive as she had never come alive before and knew she never would again. With her conscious mind she wanted to remember the experience so that when she was old and gray, she could close her eyes and think, *I know how it felt to be kissed by the one man I truly loved.*

Jonathan's kisses were the yardstick by which she would judge every other kiss from every other man in her future. None would measure up. He was the only man she would ever love this way.

Jonathan ended the kiss but still held her tight against him. Stella nestled close. It was over, useless to pretend any longer.

"I'll get Caroline," she whispered, and, using all her internal strength, she pulled away from the shelter of his arms.

"Don't say you don't love me, Stella. You just proved you do."

She placed two fingers on his lips and shook her head. "No." But even as she said the word, she wasn't sure what it was she was saying no to. Was it no she didn't love him, as she wanted him to believe, or no he shouldn't say those words, shouldn't force her to admit something she knew was better left unsaid?

"Liar," he said hoarsely.

As Stella turned away from the pain in his face, the unmistakable beat of rotor blades sounded over the gentle patter of the rain. Relentless, closer, and louder by the second.

CHAPTER TEN

Stella arrived at her Sydney apartment late that night It was another world. Just as Caroline had predicted, the dense, humid city air caught in her throat and made her cough. The traffic was deafeningly endless, the lights too bright and garish, the drivers impatient. Everything was cramped and constricted. Even her northern beach suburb, very upmarket, very sought-after, tree-filled and spacious, felt constrictive after the vast expanses of the Koologong plains.

Xavier's limo driver, who'd met her at the helipad, opened her door and carried her suitcase indoors despite her protests that she could do it herself.

"It's no problem, Stella," he said as they rode up in the elevator, "We're all glad you're back safely."

Stella dragged her attention from the depths of her misery and focused on his rugged, elderly face. "I was fine. I just needed to be by myself for a while. But thanks, Mike."

"I just wanted to tell you," he said. "I know you've had a rough time and all . . . but the staff, we were worried. Me and Alex and Joe, and even Julianne. The boss kept telling us you were having a holiday, but, well . . . you know. You went off so quickly and didn't tell anyone. There were rumors you'd been kidnapped."

She sucked in a quick, surprised gasp of air. "I'm so sorry. I had no idea you'd be worried about me! I didn't think. I told Xavier I was going, but I didn't say where. I didn't know myself at that stage. I was being selfish." She smiled and stretched up to kiss his cheek. "Thank you."

The elevator doors hissed open at the penthouse. Mike patted her on the shoulder with clumsy affection. "Alex came in and stocked up the fridge for you today. She'll be in tomorrow, she said."

Stella stepped into the foyer.

"Good night, Stella."

"Good night, and thanks, Mike."

Her smile faded as the elevator doors closed. They all cared for her. Mike and Joe, the bodyguard-cum-security man, who had worked for Xavier for years. She'd known them since she was a teenager. In Australia

Mike always drove her to official functions and concerts with Joe sitting solidly beside her.

Alex had been her secretary for the last three years, since her marriage, organizing mail, booking flights and hotels, attending to the myriad details her complicated life left no time for. She hadn't even told Alex she was going. No wonder they were all shocked and worried. They'd feel betrayed and slighted. Mike, she knew, was kind and gentle and would never chastise her, despite being almost old enough to be her grandfather. He'd always treated her with respect. She'd repaid him with worry and concern.

Being selfish wasn't a very good idea after all. Her position held responsibility. Yin and yang. The balance had to be right. Lately she'd had no balance at all.

She looked around the apartment. Xavier's decorator had done it for Mark. Elegant and arty and expensive. Certainly comfortable. But sterile. Anybody could live here. Take away the CD collection and the clothes in her closet, and it was a generic rich person's abode.

She kicked off her shoes, leaving them lying on the living room floor as she went to the kitchen to get a cup of tea started while she showered. She left dirty clothes on the bathroom floor and her suitcase lying open in her bedroom, still packed. But she had to admit to herself, it was a pitiful attempt to make this empty place seem like a home.

Stella lay in her own large bed with her future spread before her mind's eye. Under a microscope. From now on she would choose judiciously what she did. She'd spend more time writing songs and less time doing stage shows. She'd do recordings and the occasional promotional concert tour because she loved performing. She'd stay in Australia for longer periods because she wanted to be closer to her mother and she didn't want to lose her Aussieness. She didn't want to lose her accent and forget that a ute was a ute and not a pickup. She'd put a band together — her own band — and keep them together to work on her music, not just let Xavier hire different session musos as backup.

She'd have time to herself, and she'd explore other things, catch up on knowledge in areas like art and literature and history. She'd read the newspaper regularly and learn what was happening in the world. Maybe even do a university degree. She'd become a person worth knowing, a person worth loving.

And all of it should keep her mind off

him. And all of it might go partway to filling the great cavity in her soul. But until she could start on her makeover, she would have to grit her teeth and hang tough. For tonight, all she could do was curl up into a tight little ball of misery and sob.

Jonathan couldn't believe Stella had gone. He stood watching the helicopter until it completely disappeared into the gray, swirling mass that was the sky, and the sound of its engine had faded into the vast stillness. Caroline waited a short distance away, not saying a word for once. But he was glad she was there, glad she knew the best and the worst of him and he didn't have to hide anything or explain.

"I thought she might stay," he said with his back turned, his eyes searching the distant clouds in case there should be a miraculous return, a change of heart.

"She couldn't," said Caroline. "You can see why, can't you?"

"Not really."

He felt an arm slip around his waist, and he hugged her shoulders as they stood staring into the distance, lost in their own thoughts and sadness.

"Did she forgive me, do you think?" he asked eventually.

"Yes, she did."

He dropped his arm from her shoulders and turned back to the house. "Well, I suppose that's something. I don't know what I'm going to do now, Carrie."

She hurried to catch up to him. "Jon, I want to stay. For good."

"All right."

"Jon? You hear me? I want to stay permanently. I want to help you with the farm and the business. I can, you know. I've got a degree in graphic design, and I'm very good. I can help with advertising and artwork and catalogues and anything you need in that department."

Jonathan stopped and glanced at her, his interest aroused for a moment. "Can you design clothes?"

"I know someone who can. Helena De Vries. She'd leap at the chance."

Jonathan walked on. What did he care about Koolwear now? He'd spent all that energy and time pouring his heart into something that, in the end, prevented him from having the one precious thing that had come to him in a blinding moment of fate, or chance, or serendipity. A treasure above all else. Stella.

"Call her," he said.

"Jon?" They climbed the steps to the

veranda. Caroline sat in one of the cane chairs overlooking the rose garden. "I have something to tell you. Sit down."

"What is it?" She'd have nothing of interest to tell him unless she wanted to talk about Stella. But then he heard Stella's voice saying, *"Look after Caroline."* He slumped into the other chair and asked more gently, "Are you all right? Of course you can stay here. It's your home. Keith and Renata will love having you back."

"I'm pregnant."

After a stunned moment he managed to say in a reasonably normal voice, "Congratulations."

She gave a gurgle of laughter. "Really?"

His eyes widened. "Not congratulations?"

"Yes, I suppose. I'm not sure. I came home to get my head sorted out."

"The father? Your husband?" She'd married and not told her family? How she must have detested them all.

"Yes, estranged husband." Her jaw tightened. "He doesn't know, and he won't ever know. Call it a lapse of judgment on my part."

Jonathan nodded. Not tell the father? Was that fair or right? Her expression forbade further questions. Later.

"All right," he said doubtfully. Was this

what Stella had meant? She knew and was worried he wouldn't care for his sister? Another splinter lodged in his heart. How little they really knew each other.

"I meant what I said, Jon. I can work for you. I want to prove I'm not the hopeless case you thought I was. And Dad."

"We kept hoping you'd come home," he said softly. "He missed you terribly."

They sat in silence for some time until Caroline said, "What are you going to do about Stella?"

"Nothing. She doesn't want someone like me in her life. She made herself clear."

"She does. She loves you just as much as you love her. But she's not sure enough of herself, and she's not brave enough to risk it again."

"After what I did to her." He stared blankly out at the garden. "How do you know?"

"Women know. Especially pregnant ones. We have extra intuition."

He could feel her looking at him and heard the smile in her voice, but he refused to acknowledge the leap of joy her words fired in his heart. He remained silent. What did Carrie know about it? She'd known Stella for an even shorter time than he had. But they did seem to get on well, and they were both women, and women did talk about the most intimate things, he'd discovered. Just how intimate had they been?

He regarded Carrie thoughtfully. She spoke like a mature woman, not his wild little sister with the untamable nature and the thoughtless, selfish, teenage attitude. Pregnancy had forced her to accept some degree of responsibility. She'd changed in eight years. Had he?

His next words were grudging, and he hated himself for sounding churlish and, most of all, unsure. "What do you suggest I do, Carrie? Turn up at her swanky address and fight my way through all her other adoring fans and the hordes of media people who'll be hanging around her house? No, thank you."

But Carrie sat forward eagerly. "Give her time to settle down and miss you, and then do exactly that."

"And she'll say 'Get lost' and call her bodyguard."

"She won't. She loves you. She'll realize it by then."

"But how can I convince her we could make something work? Our lives are so different. I couldn't trail around after her like an accessory no matter how much I love her, and she won't come to live out here.

She told me."

"You'll have to make some changes."

"What sort of changes?" How did one change a life hemmed in by responsibility and never-ending struggle and that held the hopes and aspirations of a whole community? Stella had understood only too well. Carrie didn't. Carrie couldn't begin to understand that he couldn't just walk away from Koologong the way she had, to follow a dream, a fantasy.

"Try compromise, Jon."

"Why do you suddenly care so much about me?"

She paused and met his gaze. "I've always cared about you. After what I did to you and Dad . . ." Her voice dropped to a whisper. "I want to try to make at least somebody happy."

Jonathan sat with Carrie on the veranda talking until it got dark. Then they went inside to cook dinner and eat and talk some more. By the time they went to bed, he held a glimmer of hope that he and Stella might be able to forge a future together after all. If he could just get to see her and talk to her — and if Carrie and her pregnant woman's "intuition" were right, and Stella really did love him.

■ ■ ■ ■

"But, Stella, darling!" cried Xavier. "Why won't you even consider the offer? Imagine, your career would take off in a whole new direction." His round black eyes almost popped out of his head with consternation, and his little eyebrows danced a veritable tango across his brow.

"I'm not an actress, Xavier, I'm a singer." Stella sat implacably in her chair and swung her crossed leg casually. "There's no point in looking at the script. I don't want to make a movie. I want to record a CD of my own songs with my own band."

"It won't be a number-one seller."

"I don't care. I want to do my own music."

His expression registered his astonishment — and the recognition that she was serious and immovable.

"What happened to you out there in the wilderness?" he asked suspiciously. The creases in his brow drew together in a V. "Did you have an 'experience'?" He loaded the word with all sorts of innuendo.

"Yes. A lot of experiences, actually. I discovered to some extent what I want from my life, and, as much as I'm grateful to you and love you and respect you, Xavier, my goals are different. I'm not a teenager anymore. Thanks to you I'm financially comfortable and I can have my mother well cared for. I want to do something different."

"I know. Movies would be a good shift for you."

"I'm a singer. I want to write songs. I want to stay here. Fewer tours, Xavier. Less promo stuff. I'm tired of it"

He sighed. He flung his arms wide. "It's career suicide, darling. But what can I do?"

Stella stood up. She kissed his cheek. "I'm not stopping work, Xavier. I'll still make money for you. Just maybe a bit less."

"Not fair, Stella!" He screwed up his eyes and studied her, tapping a chubby finger against his pouting lips. "There wouldn't be a man behind all this, would there? Some country boy with a big tractor and a good line?"

The eyes popped open and the eyebrows leaped halfway up his forehead as Stella's cheeks warmed and she failed to meet his eyes. Xavier nodded. "Does he know who you are?"

He'd known her too long and too well for her to prevaricate.

"Yes, but it was nothing. And you needn't worry. He won't tell a soul. And, anyway, nothing happened."

"Stella, you should know better. Nothing needs to happen, and no man on earth would keep his mouth shut if he had a fling with Stella Starr."

"We did not have a fling!" cried Stella. "Believe me. Jonathan is just a friend. Less. An acquaintance. He means nothing to me. Anyway, after Mark, what makes you think I'd be looking for another man?"

"I know, darling. I'm sorry. You're right. That man was a complete loser, a despicable worm." This from Xavier, who'd gushed that Mark was a man in a million when they'd announced their engagement. "I'll prepare a nice little statement for the press, and you can smile and say you had a lovely break."

Xavier pulled a piece of paper across his cluttered desk. His well-fed face took on a familiar no-nonsense expression as he checked the details. Back to business. The eyebrows settled into a more regulation pose.

"I think you should attend this reception," he said. "Especially if you want to do your own music. It's the recording company, A shindig for their artists, celebrating the one hundredth hit album."

"Sure. I'll be there," said Stella. "And I'll

smile and say all the right things. Don't worry."

Despite having just been assertive, she was back in harness, and it felt like a straitjacket.

A couple of weeks later, as they sat in Stella's study going through a pile of correspondence, Alex said, "What do you think about wearing something called Koolwear?" She tossed the letter to Stella casually with a little laugh, which turned to astonishment when Stella snatched it up. "What is it? Koolwear."

"It's cotton clothing. I bought some at the factory when I was away. Out in northwestern New South Wales. They grow cotton and manufacture garments all at the same place. The business supports the whole town, pretty much."

"You seem to know a lot about it," commented Alex. "Impressive, was it?"

"Well, yes." Stella sat with the letter unread in her hand. Her mind flew to the open spaces and the gigantic, arching blue canopy of the sky, the eccentric, friendly people supporting the local hero — Jonathan. "They're working really hard to make it succeed."

"It's a good-looking proposal, well set out," said Alex. "As begging letters go."

"Caroline," murmured Stella, smiling as she studied the new logo, then skimmed through the colored brochure and catalogue accompanying the letter. She glanced quickly down to the signature at the bottom.

Colin Hill, Manager.

She frowned. Shouldn't Jonathan have signed? Wasn't he the boss? Disappointment crashed in. The first tangible contact with him since that torturous last day — the Sunday etched into her very being, branded on her soul. The look on his face as she virtually told him she didn't love him haunted her every night and most of her days. She'd lied to him again, but for his benefit, not hers, and it had torn her to shreds. Shreds she had carefully and painfully begun to cobble back together. And now this reminder.

He'd taken her at her harsh word and approached Xavier properly with a business proposition. But why hadn't he written to her, personally? Stella firmed her mouth into a straight line. Stupid question. He didn't want anything else from her. And he'd even gotten the dark, curly-haired man to sign the begging letter in case his name put her off. The company was paramount, just as Caroline had said.

"What's their stuff like?" asked Alex. "I like these pants." She pointed at the catalogue.

"The aqua blouse I wear sometimes is theirs, and I've T-shirts and a white dress as well."

"I love that one!" cried Alex. "Are you going to do it?"

"I'll have to think about it," said Stella. "What do they actually want me to do?"

"Be Miss Koolwear." Alex adjusted her glasses. "They're proposing an ad campaign. Magazines and newspapers. It'll cost them a fortune."

"I know," said Stella.

"Can they afford it?"

"I doubt it."

"Pity." Alex gathered up the proposal and placed it in a pile of other rejected mail. "I need your signature on some checks, please, Stella, just the usual. If you're going to be stuck in a recording studio for the next few weeks, I won't be able to catch you. Why can't you do it somewhere civilized instead of at that remote place?"

"Berrima's not remote! It's only an hour or so down the freeway, and the sound guy there is the best in the country. I'm really looking forward to it. It's going to be fantastic. We'll all stay together and get right

259

into it. My own songs with my own band, and I have full creative control."

Alex smiled. "Can't wait to hear it, but my kids are going to be disappointed. I told them your new CD would be in a different direction."

Stella sighed. "I know, but they might like it. Xavier's sure I'm going to lose all my fans."

"You have to do what feels right for you," said Alex firmly. "If you don't have artistic integrity, what have you got in the long run? Fans are great, but they don't keep you warm at night, and they don't have to live inside your head. They're fickle, especially the teenage market. But if you stay true to yourself, you'll please the most important person, which is your artistic self, and from there you go on to please others."

"Thanks, Alex. I think I needed to hear that. I don't have many supporters right now except my musos."

"For what it's worth, we're right behind you — Mike and me and Joe. And Julianne. Xavier, too, in his own inimitable fashion."

Stella smiled and signed the checks. The morning business continued.

After Alex had left, Stella picked up the discarded catalogue and studied the photos carefully. Would Jonathan be in one? She saw a long shot of the Koolwear factory she'd visited with him. An interior view with grinning workers, including the two girls who'd helped with her purchases. How impressed she'd been — so much so that she'd decided to take him up on his invitation. He'd known who she was all the time. It still smarted, the knowledge of his deception. She'd forgiven him, understood why he'd done it, and as Caroline had pointed out, it was a good idea he'd had. He'd just gone about it all wrong.

And that was that. But what about now? This proposal? If she accepted and became Miss Koolwear for a sum of money they could afford, what then? She'd have to see Jonathan again. Could she stand to? Would it be better or worse? Would her carefully reconstructed persona collapse into a million pieces again?

But on the other hand, could she stand not to? Sometimes at night, sleepless, she reached for the phone to call him, to hear his voice, but she couldn't bring herself to dial the number. Couldn't think of a single reason to justify restarting something that had nowhere to go. And what if he'd changed his mind?

He hadn't even signed the letter himself. He could've stuck in a little personal note, saying, *"Hi, how are you?"* Been friendly if nothing else, if he'd concluded over the intervening weeks that his undying love had been a rather embarrassing overstatement. As it probably was.

Jonathan edged the Ford into a gap in the traffic. Someone blasted a horn, but it wasn't for his benefit. A confused interstate driver had dithered too long at the intersection and missed the lights. Jonathan sat. He hated city driving. It was so time-consuming and stressful, the air fouled with exhaust fumes and grit. His lungs choked and resented every breath he took.

He glanced again at the address Caroline had given him. North Shore. Right up near Palm Beach. Beautiful and expensive area. Surrounded by thick bushland bordering on the Ku-ring-gaipark, many homes overlooked the water from private and elevated positions on the rugged coastline.

The dashboard clock said quarter to five. He had at least another hour of this stop-start crawling business. Less if the lights went his way. Should he have rung her? Probably. Turning up on her doorstep was risky but had the advantage of surprise. She wouldn't be able to hide her immediate and natural reaction. He'd be able to tell a great deal from the look in her eyes and her body language when she opened the door and saw him. She wouldn't have time to prepare a mask — or a statement.

He had a good excuse if she was cool and offhanded: He wouldn't need one if she wasn't.

He reached the motel shortly before six. Eight and a half hours of driving took their toll. He needed a shower and some food before making his attack. He chose his clothes carefully — couldn't look too much like the hick from the country here in her world.

The apartment house wasn't big. Only three stories, and, from the address, Stella's appeared to be on the top. The penthouse. There were no names in any of the little spaces for them. He buzzed the intercom with a finger shaking from nervous tension. This was it. Crunch time. This was where he discovered the shape of his future. If he failed now, he'd have to give in gracefully, go home, and get on with it. He wouldn't trail about after her, harassing her with his avowals of love until she had him arrested as a stalker. He had one shot, and this was it.

Nothing happened. He tried again and waited. She wasn't home.

Jonathan turned and walked slowly back to the car. This wasn't an unforeseen eventuality. Disappointing but not unlikely. He went to the motel and rang the private number.

"Please leave a message," said Stella's voice. His heart turned right over at the familiar, calm tone. He hung up quickly and sat staring at the phone as if it might bite him. Then he picked up the receiver and dialed again.

"Stella, it's Jonathan. From Koologong. I'm here in town for a few days, and I'd like to get together. If you would. Oh, I brought your car back. Dan fixed it, eventually." He stopped as his brain groped for more to say, but there was nothing, and the machine clicked and beeped before he could say anything else, even good-bye. Then he rang back and left the name of the motel where he was staying.

She didn't call. Not that night or the next day. She wasn't home when he went by the next morning. She was still in Sydney, he knew from reports of her movements on her fan Web site and the occasional newspaper item. There'd been a photo of her at some reception, smiling and looking unbearably gorgeous, with a rotund, swarthy man grinning by her side. He hated him.

He sat in his room and read the Yellow Pages. He discovered the agent's address in North Sydney and picked up the phone again.

"Miss Starr is recording her latest album," said the receptionist.

"Is she in Sydney? I'm a personal friend, and I was hoping to see her. I'm only in town a few days."

"I'm sorry, I can't give out personal information. But no, she's out of town."

"Can you give her a message, please?" he cried desperately. "Tell her Jonathan came to see her. He brought her car back and — and — if she wants to see him, she knows where to find him. But things have changed. He's changed. For the better. She'll understand. But say that one thing hasn't changed and never will. Can you tell her please? It's important."

"I think I got it all, sir. I'll pass it on for you."

"Thank you."

"Have a nice day."

"Thank you." Oh, sure — some nice day he'd be having. He hung up and sat on the bed with his hands dangling between his knees, head bent in despair. That bimbo wouldn't pass on his message. She dealt with crazed fans all day. Fobbed them off with bland politeness. He flopped back onto the bed.

He might as well go home. There was nothing in Sydney for him with Stella away. But what about the car? He'd brought it all this way, and she probably didn't want it back in the first place. She hadn't even mentioned it when she left. He might as well drive it home, and if she ever came through town again, she could pick it up. It could be an incentive to visit Koologong.

There was Dan's bill too, in the glove box. He could swing by and drop it into her mailbox, along with a note explaining his decision to drive back to Koologong in the Ford. He could say more or less what he'd blurted to the dopy receptionist. *"If you want it, come and get it."*

But when it came time to put words onto paper, much more poured out than he'd expected. He told her how he couldn't survive without her and how, after she flew off in the helicopter, he felt as though any meaning in his life had flown with her. He told her he was prepared to compromise and take time off from the factory to be with her in her travels if she wanted. None of it meant anything without Stella. Nothing meant anything anymore. Even the bitterness he felt toward his sister had dissolved somewhere along the line. It all seemed so unimportant. The land, the farm, the business, the town and the people in it — all suddenly empty and devoid of any value whatsoever. He told her how Caroline and Colin had taken on different aspects of the business, and he was able to loosen his grasp for the first time. How he discovered he hadn't really needed to apply a stranglehold after all, and the others were more than competent to run the place in his absence. He told her she'd made him realize nothing had any meaning for him if she wasn't part of his life, and he would accept her terms if she discovered she loved him the way he really hoped and prayed she did.

Their future was in her hands. He would accept her decision, whatever it might be.

He signed it *Your Jonathan.* And he stuffed it into an envelope, sealed it before he could change his mind, drove straight to her apartment, and dropped it in her mailbox. Then he headed for home. To wait.

But after an hour, wrestling with city traffic, depressed and numb with disappointment, he began to change his mind. The depression gave way to a slow, boiling anger, which gave way to a new determination. He'd driven hundreds of kilometers to see Stella, and see her he would. No way would

267

he go home without an answer from her lips. No way would he show his face in Koologong and the pub again without being able to say he'd given it his best shot.

He'd go to the office and see that fat bloke — her manager or agent or whatever he was — and demand to know where she was, and then he'd go and find her. Yes! Jonathan pulled into the left lane and took the next turn back toward the city. The office was in North Sydney. At least he didn't have to cross the harbor.

The receptionist was exactly as he'd imagined from her voice. Tousled black hair, lots of rings, and trendy makeup and clothes. She regarded him through blank eyes and smiled a professional smile from behind her desk. Photos of Stella and other stars smiled down from the wall behind her.

"Can I help you?"

"I'd like to see Xavier Perez-Monte, please."

"Do you have an appointment?"

"No, but it'll only take a minute of his precious time."

"I'm sorry, he's extremely busy." She punched a few buttons on her computer keyboard. "I could fit you in next Thursday."

"I want to see him now," said Jonathan. "Please."

"I'm sorry." The girl's bland expression had shifted to one of gritty determination. She was no bimbo; she was tough. But so was he.

"Please ask if he'll see me."

"May I have your name?" Her voice gained an icy edge.

"Jonathan Knight."

"And this vist would be in relation to what?" Her hand hovered above the phone.

"Stella Starr."

"Oh. You called earlier." She withdrew her hand. "I told you, we can't give out any information to fans."

"I'm not a fan. I'm a personal friend of hers."

"If you're a personal friend, then she'd have given you her personal contact details." She regarded him with a blank "got you, now go away" look on her face.

"I have them, but she's not home. I've left her a message."

"I guess that's all you can do then, isn't it?" She switched the bland smile back on.

"You don't understand. It's imperative that I see her."

"I do understand. Perfectly, Mr. Knight. Stella has men like you after her all the time."

"Where's Mr. Perez-Monte's office?"

She half rose as Jonathan started down the corridor. He flung open doors as he went, seeing startled faces briefly, hearing cries of, "Stop!" "Mr. Knight!" "Security!" and "Who are you?" following him. The final door in the corner disclosed the jackpot.

The sleek, balding man who rose from behind a large polished desk was Stella's companion in the newspaper photo. He glared at Jonathan, then past him to the gathering crowd of curious faces.

"Who is this? Where's security?"

As someone grabbed Jonathan's arms from behind, he shouted, "I have to see you! About Stella. I'm Jonathan Knight."

"And who is Jonathan Knight? Should that mean something to me?"

The grip on Jonathan tightened; voices babbled incomprehensibly behind him. He stared frantically at Xavier.

"I met her in Koologong. When she took off on her own."

"The country boy," said Xavier. Two black eyebrows headed skyward in comprehension. "Just give us a minute or two, Frank, thanks."

"You sure, Mr. Perez-Monte?"

"You don't mean me any harm, do you, Mr. Knight?"

Jonathan shook his head, readjusted his shirt, and tucked it in. Xavier nodded to Frank, who closed the door as he left.

"I'm sorry," said Jonathan, breathing hard. "I need to see Stella."

"Does she need to see you, though? That is the question."

"I think she should decide for herself."

"Mr. Knight, Stella told me a little about her trip to the outback. She mentioned you. In passing. She said she discovered quite a lot about herself and what she wanted from her life. It involved her music. A slight change of direction, which, quite frankly, I'm not all that happy with. But Stella is a talented girl. I'm inclined to trust her professional judgment."

"So am I," said Jonathan, "Which is why I need to see her. I love her. She loves me. We fell in love."

Xavier's eyebrows scaled his forehead again after a brief sojourn in their usual position. "I'm sure you do, Mr. Knight. I adore her myself. But please don't mistake Stella's naïve, generous, and lovely natural friendliness for an expression of true love. I think if that had been the case, she would have mentioned something to me on her return, don't you? It's a difficult thing to hide."

Jonathan opened his mouth but couldn't come up with a reply to counter the smooth and impervious argument.

"She mentioned me, you said?" he managed to ask.

"She did, but she also added that there was nothing of significance to report. The people she met were kind and generous, she said, but nothing happened. I did question her about her complete about-face in regard to her career. I had a movie offer waiting when she came home. Marvelous career move." Xavier beamed, and his eyebrows tap-danced now above his sparkling eyes.

"And?"

The eyebrows plummeted. "She turned it down. But I think that once she's got this album of hers finished, she'll reconsider. I'm giving her time to indulge herself, you see. She deserves it. Stella's worked hard. She's having the time of her life locked away with her own band. They're all living together and recording when they feel ready. Heaven knows what they'll produce."

"She's happy?"

"I'd say so. Yes."

"That's the main thing, then." Jonathan turned away but looked back. "Thank you for your time. I'm sorry I caused . . . I'm sorry."

Xavier came around the desk and patted his shoulder. "No hard feelings, Mr. Knight. Stella is a lovely woman, and it's no wonder you fell for her. We all do. Meeting her so unexpectedly in the flesh must have been quite a shock." He chuckled and walked with Jonathan down the corridor. Curious faces peered at them from open doorways. They reached the reception desk.

"Amber, give Mr. Knight a copy of Stella's latest CD, please. Autographed."

"Certainly." She produced the CD and handed it to Jonathan with a brittle smile.

"I'm sorry about earlier, Amber," said Jonathan. "It was — I'm sorry."

"No problem, Mr. Knight. Good-bye."

"Good-bye."

Jonathan shook Xavier's proffered hand, then hurried out through the frosted-glass doors to the foyer, where he gave up waiting for the lift and ran down ten floors to ground level. He burst onto the street and stood panting on the footpath with moisture dampening his eyes and people giving him curious glances as they pushed by. He was still clutching the CD with Stella's eyes smiling sexily at him over a feathery fan. He drew a deep, shuddery breath, then closed his eyes briefly.

A teenaged girl came along the street in

hipster jeans and a midriff-revealing top, earphones in place. He stuck out his hand with the CD and said, "Here. Autographed CD of Stella Starr. It's yours."

She stared at him in wary surprise and removed the earphones. He thrust it at her again with a forced smile. His manner must have reassured her, because she took it and called, "Cool, thanks," as he strode away toward his car.

CHAPTER ELEVEN

Stella raised her glass to the musicians crowded into the recording studio.

"We did it. Well done, everyone. Thank you." She was rewarded by applause and whistles as they raised their own glasses and joined in the congratulations.

"It's gonna be a winner, Stella," said the bass player. "I can feel it in the old bones."

"I don't care if it isn't. This was something I really wanted to do. For myself."

The recordings had gone even better than Stella could have hoped. She'd chosen musicians she knew and respected, and they'd leaped at the chance to create something new together. The song she'd written sitting under the tree while Jonathan and Grant fixed the pump had evolved into the title track, "Please Yourself."

They'd been working solidly for three weeks in the small country town of Berrima. The locals accepted the influx with casual nonchalance, unfazed by Stella's occasional appearance in the street or at the shops. The press had lost interest as well after her initial return. She wasn't drunk or stoned or mad, she wasn't being outrageous, and she wasn't having an affair with another star, or pregnant. She wasn't very interesting at the moment. She was working.

The bass player brought his wife and small children, two others brought girlfriends to stay weekends, and the large house Stella had rented for the duration became a communal home. Everything helped take her mind off Jonathan. Nearly.

When she was singing and working, it was fine. When they stopped for meals or sat around in the garden having an hour off, or played board games in the evenings, or went for bush walks to clear their heads, it wasn't. Jonathan wasn't there. Jonathan would never be there. Jonathan was where he belonged, doing what he knew best, doing what he wanted. And that was right.

But it hurt. And she missed him so much sometimes, she thought she wouldn't be able to get out of bed in the morning, the day seemed to stretch so endlessly ahead. But she did, and she dragged herself to the kitchen for breakfast, plastered on a smile, and gradually the warmth and camaraderie of the band and the others in the house went partway to smoothing over the rawness and the intense loneliness.

What would she do now? Now the recording was completed. Stella sipped the celebratory champagne and smiled and laughed, because she was proud of what they'd done, but it was hollow pleasure. Sure, she had the mixing to do with Roger, the expert recording engineer, and all the other bits and pieces connected with producing a CD, but it would all be done in Sydney, now that they had the master tape. She'd have to go home. Alone.

"I've loved being here with you," she said to the room at large. "I want this band to stay together, guys."

"Sure thing, Stella," they said. She knew they meant it, but it wasn't enough anymore, the way she'd imagined it might be.

They all packed up the next day and drove back to Sydney separately, the way they'd arrived. Stella drove her black Porsche with the personalized license plates. As she loaded her red suitcase into the trunk, it suddenly occurred to her for the first time that she'd left her other car, the little white Ford, in Dan's dubious care in Koologong.

She hadn't paid him! What an example to set. How disgusted must they be with the big star who blows into town, sponges off the local hero, breaks his heart, and clears out without even paying her bills? Stella's face glowed with embarrassment. She couldn't go back. She'd ask Alex to fix it. Alex could contact the factory and get Dan's phone number, then send him a check. As for the car? Well, she'd ask Dan to sell it. Or tell him to keep it. If he'd actually managed to fix the thing.

That hot, uncomfortable evening flashed vividly before her mind as she drove. Jonathan walking with her to the garage, finding it locked. His surprisingly accurate assessment of her state of mind. But he knew who she was even then, and he didn't say a word! The way he'd looked at her almost made her cry. The unexpected tenderness, and the invitation to dinner coming at the best possible moment, saving her from begging Leo to let her stay.

Leo would have. He was a kind man. It was Jonathan's plan and Jonathan who had made such a big thing of insisting she stay the weekend. A stray tear rolled down Stella's cheek. She sniffed viciously and scraped her hand across her eyes. He'd probably told Leo not to let her stay on credit, knowing she was perfectly capable of paying.

She couldn't show her face there ever again, not with humiliation still smoldering in the recesses of her mind. He didn't love her, no matter what he'd said and what he thought at the time. Time itself had revealed that fact. He'd neither written nor called. He'd even organized Colin to sign the business letter. *Finito!*

An overpowering urge to see her mother rose unbidden from the depths — she didn't question why. Instead of going straight home when she reached Sydney, Stella took the turnoff to a quiet, leafy, North Shore suburb housing the exclusive nursing home.

She sat holding her mother's pale, soft hand for half an hour. The woman smiled and occasionally asked gently peculiar questions and invited Stella to drink a cup of coffee even as they sat drinking tea. It was restful in a way. Her mother was still relatively youthful and attractive. Snippets of her once-lively personality remained.

"I have a daughter, you know," she said as Stella prepared to leave.

"I know," she replied, pathetically delighted by this display of awareness.

"She sings like an angel. Her name is . . ." Her mother frowned. "Who did you say you were? Would you like a cup of coffee? They'll bring some. They're very nice here." She peered around vaguely, then settled back into her chair with her eyes closed.

Stella leaned down and kissed the soft cheek. "Bye, Mum," she murmured.

When she finally reached the penthouse, it was late afternoon. Alex had left a pile of mail on the table, the answering machine had a couple of messages for her, and the rooms were just as empty and soulless as before.

She flung open the double sliding door to the balcony, letting cool evening air sweep the staleness out toward the ocean. The fridge yielded an unopened bottle of orange and mango juice. She poured herself a glass before tackling the chore of unpacking yet again. The phone rang. She paused as the machine answered.

"Hello, Stella darling. Are you home?"

She picked up. "Hi, Xavier. I just walked in."

"How did it go?"

"Wonderful. Have you spoken to Roger?"

"Yes. He said the same thing. Maybe I was wrong." He sighed as though that possibility was at the same time unprecedented and unlikely.

"I want to tour the band," she said. "Smaller venues for starters. Maybe festivals."

"Come in tomorrow, and we'll talk. Just wanted to check that you were home safely. I called earlier."

That explained at least a couple of the messages. Not many people had this private number. Stella hung up and pressed the play-messages button.

Alex. "Thought I might catch you before you left, but I haven't. No probs. Have a ball."

An open line and the click of a hang-up.

Then, "Stella, it's Jonathan. From Koologong. I'm here in town for a few days, and I'd like to get together. If you would. Oh, I brought your car back. Dan fixed it eventually." Silence for a few moments. *Beep.*

Stella stood frozen. When? When had he called? She'd been away for weeks. His was the second — no, third — message. The message timer said Tuesday, 9:13 P.M. Which Tuesday?

His voice again. "Sorry. Not thinking. I'm at the Ocean View Motel in Newport." He gave the number and hung up.

She stared, wild-eyed, at the answering machine. The next message was Xavier, and the next. They were today's. She had no way of knowing when Jonathan had called. She slammed her glass onto the table, slopping juice heedlessly in the process. Her fingers

281

could barely grasp the receiver as she dialed the number. Had she remembered it correctly?

"Ocean View Motel," said a man's voice.

"Do you have a Jonathan Knight staying. A guest?"

"One moment please." She heard the click of computer keys. "No, I'm sorry, we don't."

"He may have been there sometime in the last three or four weeks."

Silence again. "Yes, he was here just over two weeks ago. He only stayed one night."

"Thank you."

She stood with hands clenched by her sides, heart pounding, mind whirling. He'd come to see her. He'd brought the car all the way from Koologong. Where was it? Xavier hadn't mentioned anything about either him or the car, so he couldn't have contacted the agency.

She replayed the message. His voice sent shivers down her spine, made her breath catch in her throat. Here for a few days, he said. He'd only stayed one. Why? Because she wasn't home? Because he hated the city and couldn't bear to stay longer? His business was in the city, and he moved to another motel? She could go mad like this. Only one way to find out what was going on. Call Jingaluck and ask him herself.

Caroline answered. She sounded cool and reserved.

"How are you?" asked Stella through her nervousness. "Getting larger?'

"Not much showing yet. How are you, Stella?" Why did that sound like a loaded question?

"I'm fine. Caroline, is Jonathan there?" She hesitated, then said in a rush, because Caroline didn't answer immediately, "It's about my car."

"No, he's not home yet."

"Oh. Will you tell him I rang, please?"

Caroline breathed deeply into the phone. "I don't think it's a very good idea. He's just gotten himself back together after his trip to Sydney." She paused and then cried, "Why didn't you call him back, Stella?"

Stunned, Stella blinked and choked as a rush of tears threatened to engulf her. "I only just got home a few minutes ago. I've been away for nearly four weeks, recording. Caroline, of course I would've called him. I didn't know he'd been here. I rang straight-away."

"That's what I told him, but he's been really quiet and difficult to live with since he got back. I think it's best if your name doesn't come up."

"I'm sorry."

"Yeah, well, he'll get over it," said Caroline brutally. "What do you want to do about your car?"

Stella matched the tone. "Sell it. I have my own here in Sydney. It wouldn't have been very inconspicuous traveling about in a Porsche with *Stella* on my plates." She forced a laugh. "I'll have my assistant send the paperwork and a check for Dan. I feel bad about not paying him."

"I can imagine," said Caroline in a return to her cold voice.

"I have to go." More tears fought their way to her eyelids.

"Good-bye, Stella."

"Take care."

The connection clicked in her ear. Now Caroline hated her too. Jonathan didn't want her. He just wanted to offload her car. Doing Dan a favor. He'd probably brought the bill with him as well.

Stella slumped into one of the dining chairs. A pool of spilled juice spread across to the pile of letters Alex had left. She pushed them away from the flood, and the neat stack toppled and cascaded across the table. Some landed in the wet, and she grabbed them quickly, glancing at the envelopes. One had no stamp — hand-addressed and delivered. She sometimes got those from keen fans who discovered her home address.

But this handwriting was familiar. Her heart swelled to bursting. Jonathan's neat, sloping script, the same as in the notebook from the glove compartment of his ute. The one she'd torn pages from to write her song under the tree that hot, happy day. Her hands trembled even more as she carefully slipped a finger under the flap and withdrew the densely packed sheets. He *had* written to her. Pages and pages.

She read eagerly, gobbling down the words, sometimes stopping to wipe away tears. When she'd finished, she went through it all again, slowly and thoroughly, savoring every nuance, every phrase, every expression, hearing his voice in her head as she read, hearing him pour out his love and his desperation. The desperation and heartbreak that matched hers completely. He hadn't forgotten her any more than she had him. By the time she laid the final page down carefully, her mind was made up. Jonathan had laid his heart and soul bare before her. She had to do the same for him.

Clutching the precious letter in her hand, Stella headed for the bedroom. Early to bed tonight. Tomorrow she had a long drive ahead of her.

■ ■ ■ ■

Jonathan sat in the bar at a table by himself. At the back. He didn't want company. Everyone knew that now. They'd generally given up trying to cheer him with jokes and small talk. They left him alone to sit nursing his drink for the best part of the evening. He didn't have much choice of where to go with his sorrow. Not that it made any difference where he was. The heartbreak followed relentlessly. Home was as bad as the pub. She'd been in both places, plus the factory and in the ute. She was with him everywhere.

But at home were Keith and Renata, maintaining a tactful silence, keeping to themselves. And Carrie with her sympathetic smile, reminding him constantly of a woman's softness and a woman's scent with her woman's clothing on the clothesline and her woman's things in the bathroom. Carrie, who in a few short hours had become closer to Stella than he had in a couple of days and a lifetime of adoration. Carrie, who'd prevented him following in his father's footsteps and becoming a drunk. Although he'd never wanted to take that path; he'd seen only too clearly the consequences. Drink wasn't a solution.

No. What he really wanted was to wallow in peace. To sit and stare and not move, not have to make decisions. Leo allowed him that luxury. Leo let him sit with his one untouched glass of beer growing warm and flat for hours at a time. Even Grandpa kept his opinions to himself and slept in a chair on the other side of the room. Sometimes it was just the two of them in the afternoons. He didn't come in every day. Just when he needed to get away from the factory and the sight of the rows and rows of cotton plants. He almost hated them now. They'd become a constant reminder of his responsibilities, a yoke around his neck, holding him here just when he'd discovered he needn't stay. Because where else could he go?

Between them, Caroline and Colin had developed a very competent working relationship. Carrie's friend Helena had proven an innovative and talented designer with boundless enthusiasm and ideas for a wider range of garments. Keith could concentrate on running the farming side. Jonathan was general manager, but he already had a team of workers in place who knew what to do. He'd become the overseer of a well-running machine. He couldn't summon up the interest anymore. There was no point to any of it.

The trip to Sydney had completely finished him off. He'd driven the hundreds of kilometers home like a zombie, stopping only when he realized the Ford needed petrol. He forgot to eat and arrived at Jingaluck in the dark. He ignored Carrie's worried face and persistent questions and went straight to his room, where he collapsed onto his bed to sleep for twelve hours.

The next day was even worse, because upon waking he discovered that the horrendous events had in fact been real and not, as he'd thought in the twilight moments before becoming fully conscious, a nightmare. He remembered the letter he'd written in a mad moment of anguish and wished with all his heart he hadn't, wished he'd come to his senses before he dropped the massive outpouring of love and emotion into her mailbox.

Gradually over the course of the next couple of days Carrie was able to garner small fragments of the story. First she was angry, then resigned; then she stopped mentioning Stella at all. He knew she was disappointed in her assessment of someone she'd thought could be a friend. And upset at her own part in pushing him to go to

Sydney, assuring him of Stella's love. Shocked into silence by her own failed intuition.

But Stella, out of her depth and in need of assistance, was obviously very different from Stella Starr in her own environment. Carrie wasn't to blame. Three weeks later, and still no word from the woman. Didn't even want her car. How rich and careless did you have to be not even to think of paying the person who'd repaired it? How she must have chuckled over his words — before she filed them in the bin with all the other besotted fan mail.

Jonathan sat and thought and hated himself for thinking such things about her because he loved her, and no matter what she'd done or not done, that fact would never change. He loved her, and he couldn't conceive of a world where that was not the case.

He hoped with all his heart she was happy.

Leo clumped out of the back room with a tray and began stacking clean glasses under the counter. The outer door opened and closed, and he looked up. Jonathan saw him squint at the newcomer, then a grin spread across his face.

"G'day, love. What brings you here?"

Jonathan turned his head idly. Any newcomer to Koologong was worthy of mild curiosity. A woman paused just inside the door, but the glare from outside made it difficult to distinguish her features. Then she moved forward.

She was beautiful. Thick honey-blond hair curled and waved about her shoulders. The skin of her bare arms and throat was tanned golden brown, and she moved with the lithe grace of a dancer. She wore blue jeans and silly high-heeled sandals and a casual white blouse. A Koolwear blouse. Jonathan's heart stopped beating. The room froze. She hadn't noticed him sitting quietly in the rear corner. The woman was beautiful and very, very familiar.

"Hello, Leo." Her voice made his heart leap and bound, beating like a voodoo drum.

"Never thought we'd see you back here," said Leo. "Like a drink?"

"No, thanks. I'm looking for Jonathan." Was it his imagination, or did her voice catch on his name? Did it sound tense and almost tentative? "They told me at the factory he might be here."

Leo nodded in his direction, and she turned and saw him. He caught a glimpse of Leo disappearing through the door to the kitchen behind her; then she was all he could possibly take in. She glowed and shone with loveliness. He couldn't believe she was so beautiful, even more perfect than he remembered. He couldn't believe she was here. Jonathan sat and stared. If he spoke, she might disappear.

"Hello," she said at last, and her voice was tentative, and it did catch.

"Hello." The word barely made it past his lips. He didn't dare blink.

She stepped closer. "I'm sorry I missed you in Sydney. I was away recording. I didn't know . . ." Her voice trailed away.

Stella looked down at the floor, then glanced at Grandpa asleep in an armchair by the window. Jonathan had hardly reacted at all. He wasn't pleased to see her. She'd made another dreadful mistake. But the letter . . .

"I read your letter," she said softly.

Jonathan said nothing, but he pushed the chair back with a scraping rasp and stood up. Had he heard? She watched him come toward her, tall and imposing. Breathtakingly wonderful. His expression told her nothing. She was too late. She shivered. Her hands were clammy, and she rubbed the palms against her jeans.

"I wanted you to know how I felt," he said hoarsely. "But I guess you already knew.

And you didn't care."

His eyes seemed to bore into her. Stella stood her ground. If he was angry, it wouldn't be surprising, but she had to know. She'd come too far to back out now. She'd driven virtually nonstop since early in the morning for this. Was there nothing left here for her?

She cleared her throat. "I'm sorry," she said. "I only got home yesterday."

"Yesterday?"

Stella nodded. "I've been recording an album. In Berrima."

"I know."

Jonathan frowned, then his expression softened, and he stepped even closer. So close, she could feel the warmth of his body and smell his intoxicating, special smell. She wanted to lean in and rest her head on his chest so much, it hurt. She wanted his arms around her. But he kept them hanging loosely by his sides.

He stared at her. "You flew here?"

"I drove."

"Drove yourself?"

Stella nodded, hypnotized by his eyes, paralyzed by their nearness.

"Why?"

"You know why."

"No. I don't." His voice was harsher than

she'd ever heard. "Tell me."

"I want to know if you still feel the same," she managed to say. He was staring at her with an expression she couldn't understand. Was it anger? Disgust?

"Jonathan!" she cried in dismay. "Jonathan?" Her eyes flooded with tears. It was too late. The love he had poured so passionately into his letter had died of neglect, stagnated, and perhaps even turned to dislike. "Don't you love me anymore? I can understand if you don't, if you thought I didn't care. I just had to know. That's why I came. Caroline said —"

He interrupted then. "Caroline?"

"She said when you came home after Sydney, you were so upset, she thought it best if my name wasn't mentioned."

"When did you call her?"

"Yesterday. Last night. After I got home and got your message. Before I read the letter."

Jonathan gripped her shoulders tightly with both hands. He stared into her eyes. "You want to know if I feel the same about you? If I still love you? That's why you drove all day to get here? All by yourself?"

She nodded.

"Tell me why it's suddenly so important to you, Stella."

She pulled away from his grasp. "Don't you know?"

Why was he doing this to her? Surely he could guess. Maybe he wanted to hear her say what he'd said to her so many times so he could tell her he'd changed his mind and watch her suffer.

He flung his arms into the air. "How could I know? I don't know what you think. I only know what you say and what you do. And you told me you didn't love me clearly enough, right after I'd told you I loved you. I told you so many times. And you left so fast . . . I loved you, Stella."

"But not enough to leave Koologong," she flung back at him. "I'm sorry. I shouldn't have come. I thought . . ."

"What? What did you think?"

"What you wrote . . . have you changed your mind?" She couldn't help it; her voice broke, the words choked in her throat.

"Changed my mind?" He took a step forward. He raised a hand slowly and caressed her cheek. Stella closed her eyes. Her body trembled under his touch, featherlight and exciting, so exciting she could barely breathe. She pressed her cheek against his fingers.

She opened her eyes to meet his gaze. "Have you?" she whispered. "I drove all the way here, hoping you hadn't." A tear escaped and ran down from the corner of her eye. He caught it with his thumb.

"Have you changed your mind?" He cupped her face gently in both his palms.

"Yes, about a lot of things, but not about the main one. I'm clearer about that than anything. I love you, Jonathan, and I want to be with you. If you still want me. Do you? Am I too late?"

"What a question," he whispered as he slid his hand around the back of her neck under her hair to draw her close.

Stella melted into his embrace and his kiss. Everything she'd ever wanted was here in this man in this moment. He held her as if he'd never let her go, and she didn't want him to. Ever.

Eventually a noise from the outer door made them draw apart, starry-eyed and breathless at the wonder of what they'd discovered and nearly lost. Leo's voice called, "All right, everyone! They've got it sorted."

Stella glanced at Jonathan and just had time to register his amused expression before the door burst open. Half if not the whole population of Koologong poured into the pub. Faces from the factory where she'd stopped to enquire after Jonathan, Keith and Renata grinning like idiots, and there was Caroline, with a smile so wide, her face might crack in two. Judy and Grant laughed and clapped. Doreen fluttered. Dan grinned. Leo charged forward and slapped Jonathan on the back.

"Beauty, mate!" he cried.

"I should have known," Stella said.

Carrie flung her arms around her. "Thank goodness. I couldn't believe I'd gotten you so wrong."

"I got me wrong," said Stella. "You got me right."

"Doesn't matter now," Leo said. "You and Jon've got each other."

"Champagne on Jonathan," called Colin. He turned to Stella. "I hope you're going to take him away and get him out of our hair every now and again."

"If he wants to come, I'd love it, but I sort of planned to live here some of the time." She looked at Jonathan questioningly. He squeezed her hand.

"Why on earth would you want to do that?" asked Leo, handing her a glass of champagne.

"It's Jonathan's home, and it's beautiful. I can write songs out here. I've already recorded the one I wrote out by the pump." She smiled at Jonathan. "It's called 'Please

Yourself.' "

He leaned down, his breath tickling her ear as he whispered, "And will you?"

Stella stretched up on tiptoe and whispered, "I'd rather we pleased each other."

Grandpa's voice rose above the roar of celebrations. "This is my pub! And there's Margie! What a girl! Give us a song, darl."

ABOUT THE AUTHOR

Elisabeth Rose lives in Australia's capital, Canberra. She completed a performance degree on clarinet, traveled Europe with her musician husband, and returned to Canberra to raise two children. Twenty-two years ago she began practicing Tai Chi, and now teaches classes in that as well as teaching and playing clarinet. Reading has been a lifelong love, writing romance a more recent delight.

Outback Hero is Elisabeth Rose's fourth book for AVALON. *Stuck, Coming Home,* and *The Right Chord* are also available.

The employees of Thorndike Press hope you have enjoyed this Large Print book. All our Thorndike, Wheeler, and Kennebec Large Print titles are designed for easy reading, and all our books are made to last. Other Thorndike Press Large Print books are available at your library, through selected bookstores, or directly from us.

For information about titles, please call:
  (800) 223-1244

or visit our Web site at:
  http://gale.cengage.com/thorndike

To share your comments, please write:
  Publisher
  Thorndike Press
  295 Kennedy Memorial Drive
  Waterville, ME 04901